THE TRIBE

I0571831

BEDTIME STORIES AND DREAMS

Grandfather's bedtime stories aren't as innocent as they seem, but those dark tales could be a young man's only hope. Now to transform the onset of events he must alter the past.

DREAM KILLER Book I

THE TRIBE Book II

RIM STONE Book III

AWAKE ASLEEP DREAMING DEAD

The driver's focus is on the disappearing center line. Then the sun begins to rise, and it's like nothing he's seen before, he stops to admire it and takes a picture. He's tired, closes his eyes, and as the last word rolls off his lips, at this last flutter of time, the driver will choose to be awake, asleep, dreaming or dead.

ExPRESSION

John Bird Ray discovers that writing a book is an absorbing journey—especially if you're part of the story. Swirls of ink take him on a fantasy linked with reality. A reflection of the world twisting and turning on the roller coaster of time.

THE POETRY OF FOOD & DRINK

Poetry for the connoisseur. In one's lifetime there are various opportunities, and for whatever reason, some are seized, others rejected. On occasion, we heartly greet or labor to befriend each other, but what all of us have in common is a need and love for - Food & Drink.

FENCES

Poems that explore the experience and challenge of life. One step at a time, day by day, month by month, year by year. Journey through the fences of time.

INFLEXATION

Puzzles put together to convey ideas, feelings, and emotions with words from the experience of living life. Words to create images that capture emotions.

ARE YOU CASABLANCA

It happens when seeking love and romance. A warm feeling fills the heart, alive with uncontrollable energy, lifting the spirit and soul. It abides as a smile or a twinkle in the eye for all to see.

WARBLINGS

The following is an echo of something I once read - Our heart is an incarnation of thought which turns into an idea again and again as ice becomes water and gas. The mind precipitates this votile essence as a forever escaping state of free imagination.

JOHN SIWICKI

ISBN13 978-0-9792622-5-8

This novel is a work of fiction.

Published by **SLABYPRESS**

W25952 State Road 95 Arcadia, WI 54612 U.S.A.

For publication data or information

contact the publisher slabypress@yahoo.com

Contact author at: infojsiwicki@gmail.com

www.jsiwicki.blog

www.jsiwicki.com

Technical, cover, and book design by JBS

THE TRIBE

THE

TRIBE

Bedtime Stories and Dreams
Memories of Michael Colt -book II

JOHN SIWICKI

-Sleep to dream, die so dead-
-Wake to live a memory left in one's head-

JOHN SIWICKI

MOVING

"I first saw a dead human at a funeral when I was seven years old."

It was an answer to a question that just popped into Michael Colt's head while following a hearse in traffic.

What happens to all of the knowledge that a person accumulates over a lifetime? I think it has weight, value, just like gold.

Are dreams and memories lost forever, or are they just left floating in the air waiting to be collected.

Michael Colt wasn't sure why these thoughts came to mind on this day, at this time. He parked his car and climbed the creaky stairs of the three-story possibly hundred year old house. There was muffled music playing as he stood in front of the door. After fiddling with his keys a moment he unlocked, and walked into the 2nd floor apartment he'd just recently rented. This is the apartment where he moved with his longtime sweetheart, Sue.

Moving or going to a new place is almost the same as moving to another city or country. Because moving anywhere emboldens exploring a new location, and is needed to find out what goes on, who lives there, and what's useful. We talk to people, collect information, and make conclusions.

After being met with blasting musical vibrations floating through the air, he thought, *She's home I guess*, then yelled over the pulsating guitar, bass, and drums echoing off the walls, and through the halls, "What's the name of that song?"

He repeated the question while listening to the music, standing in the kitchen as it bellowed from the living room, then paused a moment trying to remember the name of the song. As he looked up noticed a crack in the ceiling, and thought, *Was that crack there when we first looked at this place?*

He threw his coat over a chair by the kitchen table. "I really like that group."

"Smells like Teen Spirit," Sue said from the living room.

"What?"

"Smells like Teen Spirit," Sue repeated and yelled.

"Do you think it's too loud? I can turn it down."

"Has anyone complained?"

"Not, yet," she said.

"Probably okay, then," he said. "I haven't heard that one for a long time," then he opened the fridge, and looked over what was sitting there.

Left-overs, he thought, *Not tonight, don't feel like eating that*, and decided to take out a bottle of beer. He closed the fridge, and looked toward the living room. "How was your day?" There was no answer from the living room. "Sue?" Still no reply. "Sue?" he repeated.

Michael walked into the living room, saw Sue dressed in a white tank top and jean shorts stretched out on the black leather sofa. One arm under her head, the other across her waist, legs crossed and her feet propped up on a Scooby-Doo pillow. She was glowing.

"Hey," he said. "You look comfortable. How was your day?"

Sue smiled at Michael, then said, "Fine, and how was your day? You just get back from Hungry Point?"

"Yeah, helped Moses build a stone fireplace today for a guy who just bought a hobby farm near there," then he looked around the room and noticed how some things had changed. "Looks like you've got everything put away, and under control," he said, while eyeing a pile of neatly folded and stacked empty cardboard boxes in the corner.

"You've unpacked and put away everything pretty fast. Amazing, you should be a professional mover."

"I'm professional in everything I do."

"Well, I agreed, you certainly are that." He leaned down, kissed, then wrapped his arms around Sue, and held her close in a tight grip. "Are you happy?" he whispered in her ear.

"Yes, I am," she whispered back, then they were quiet staying there unshaken on the sofa. Sue was grinning like she knew something and wanted to blurt it out, but held back for the full and long-lasting effect of surprise she expected would come later, after what she knew was revealed.

Michael asked, "You okay?" completely rapt in curiosity at her behavior. "What's going on?" He continued watching her, then said. "I know that look. You're dying to tell me something. What is it? I can tell you're up to something or know something by that look on your face."

Sue fixed a laser gaze on Michael, smiled again while grabbing her long brown hair, pulled it back into a pony tail, and giggled. "Yes, everything's unpacked, and almost all done. About all put away, too, just some odds and ends left. Not sure about those things over there. You know, on what to keep or toss. Why don't you look through that pile of stuff and see if there's anything you want. It's mostly your stuff anyway."

"Okay, I have a look later. My old stuff is not so important. Now tell me what else happen today?" he asked. "I know there's more on your mind than unpacking boxes and looking through some old stuff to ditch. You seem like you know something that I don't, and I want to know what that something is. I'll get it out of you."

"I just got back a little while ago too," she said.

"Yeah, back from where? You didn't say anything about going out today."

"For an appointment I made a few weeks ago."

"Appointment?" his faced perplexed in an angling shape. What for? How many weeks ago? Two?" Don't remember you mentioning anything about making any appointments." Michael sat on the end of the sofa near her feet like a little kid on the first day of school, feeling totally out of the loop, lost, and no idea what was going to happen next. "Appointment," he said again, "a few weeks ago. What's this all about? You're making this sound so serious. Come on, tell me what the appointment was for. I want to know."

"I have some spectacular news," she said with a grin that conveyed endless happiness. "It's something that will especially change our lives, along with our family and friends lives forever."

He stood, leaned over, kissed her cheek, then sat down again. "This is sounding like it's going to be very good news. Okay, I'll bite, tell me, or give me some clue, hint, something. What's the news? I've seen you like this before, and know you want to blurt it out. I just know it. I feel like the river's ready to burst the dam."

"It's been the most surprising day," she said, "an unbelievably fantastic day. And you're right, the dam will burst, and we're starting a new journey of our life."

"An unbelievable surprising fantastic day? A new journey? Now we're getting somewhere, and I like what I'm hearing."

"Not sure you're ready to hear this news yet?"

"Come on, what happened? Did you find something you thought you'd lost while unpacking? Wait that's not it, you said, an appointment. It's got something to do with the appointment you had."

"You're right, didn't find anything, and you're right again, it has something to do with the appointment today, and you went somewhere today."

He reached over and caressed the soles of her feet, then his hands with a mind of their own made their way around her ankles, and danced up along the side of her legs. The pleasure trip continued farther up her inner thigh massaging in short movements, softly, then walked his fingers up her athletic and tight muscular body. Sue worked hard to keep herself in shape, exercising and doing yoga almost every day at home and the gym.

***

Growing up as a teenager Sue was a human magnet, and even though Hungry Point was a small town, boys at the small school near Hungry Point followed her all over the place. Her groupies couldn't get enough of how she looked, spoke, or moved. This continued until she met Michael who when a child between one and three years old, moved to into town to live with his grandfather.

According to the story told to him by grandfather, Poppi, his parents were killed in a car accident, but that story always changed, so he wasn't sure what to believe. At school he was one of the groupies who followed and floated on air trying to get Sue to notice him. Finally, when she did, their relationship clicked and they were inseparable. A new age had begun for them, and they had a bond that would never break, at least so they thought.

***

Sue sat up, and grabbed Michael's arms. "Okay, I'll tell you." She looked at him with a new determination he'd never seen. "Are you ready?"

"Yes, wait," Michael sat up straight, picked up the bottle of beer, took a swig, and moved into a comfortable position. "Okay, I'm ready. Lay it on me. What happened?" Then he paused a moment with a worried look changing his face and asked, "Wait, nothing's wrong is it?"

From her jean pocket a piece of paper emerged, then she waved it in front of Michael's face and brushed it across his nose. "Surprising or maybe a miracle is the only word I can think of that describes this."

At first his head jerked back and away, then as she continued to wave the paper, he leaned in closer. "What is that? Looks like a picture? Let me see," he said, and tried grabbing the paper, but she held on to it. Michael grabbed Sue at the waist and she laughed as he tickled her, but she wouldn't let it go of the paper. His hands moved from her stomach to her hands trying to weaken her with more tickling.

"Fine, fine," a smiled appeared and she laughed again. "I give up. Okay, okay, I give up."

"What is it?" Michael said. "You're smiling, and so happy. You must have some really good news?" She handed him the picture, he looked at it, then a smile appeared. "Is this what I think it is?"

"Yes," she said, and lightly punched his shoulder. "You big lug. I'm going to be a mommy, and you're going to be a daddy."

"When's this happening? How long have you been expecting? When's the due date?"

"It's written there on the side of the picture," she said.

He glanced down scanning what was written. "December 25th. That's a good time of year, and will be quite the Christmas present. Does anyone else know? You tell anyone other than me? Am I the first to know?"

"You're the first," she said. "I want to tell my parents and Kick tonight or tomorrow."

"Okay, but you do all of talking," Michael said.

"I don't think your newly found parents care for me. Kick's okay, we get along. I talk with him when I stop by the bar in Hungry Point, and have known him for as long as I can remember. He's a good guy."

"I think my parents like you," Sue said. "Dad offered you a job. Got this apartment for us."

"Your mom's fine, and friendly. It's your dad I'm just not sure about. And I don't know why we're living here in this apartment he set us up in. I think we could've found a place on our own."

"He thinks he just feels that he has to help in some way. Why do you think they don't like you?"

"Because he asks too many questions, and always looks at me like I've given the wrong answers. I'm not comfortable around him. On top of that he's got that German twangy accent that makes me feel like I'm guilty of something. For some reason his accent affects how I feel, or maybe could be it's something else. I don't know. It's probably just me."

"I think you're exaggerating, he likes you," Sue said. "How can his accent mean he doesn't like you? Only just met them. Give it some time and they'll grow on you. Before you know it you'll be talking about the good old days."

"The good old days? I'm not that old. It's not just his accent, it's him. But okay, whatever you say, maybe it's just me. I'll try to warm up to him." Michael got excited and yelled, "Wow! I've got a million things going through my head. We made a baby."

"You're happy?"

"Happy?" he said. "I can't wait till December. When do we find out if we're having a boy or girl?"

"After the next appointment we should be able to find out, and know that if we want, but surprises are nice, I think. At least that's the way it used to be."

"Maybe you're right, and we should wait until the babies born to know." Michael became serious and looked at Sue overwhelmed with deep conviction. "What about getting married?"

"Well, now that you bring it up," she said. "What do you think? Should we take the leap? I think family and friends would be happy."

"Is a small wedding okay with you?" Michael asked.

"I'm sure my parents will want to help as much as possible with arranging some things," Sue said. "I know they'll want to invite all friends and relatives on both sides, and it would be a good chance for everyone to meet and get to know each other better."

"Your parents are pretty rich from what I can tell, money seems to be no problem," Michael said. "They invited you to live with them, until they found out about me. Your dad even offered to buy you a house."

"I'm sure they'll want to put on a big bash, but don't want them to feel they have to pay for everything. This place is okay, until we need one that's bigger."

"Well, that might be sooner then we thought with the new arrival coming."

"Things will work out," Sue said. "Finding this place did. Their friend owns this house, and said we can stay as long as we like."

"Only met them a couple of times, and like I said, can't help getting the feeling your dad doesn't like me. Maybe it's because I turned down his job offer."

"I don't know them that well either. You know, finding out that I have parents who are alive after all this time was quite a shock, and puzzled me, especially the way it happened. But sounds like the job at his company's always there for you. Don't think he wants to force you into anything. Just think about it, and who knows, maybe you'd like it."

"I have my own business," Michael said, "and don't know what I'd do at your dad's company. He runs some kind of IT research computer company from what I've heard when we met last. I know so little about the kind of work his company does, and definitely not enough to just start doing working there without some massive training. I think I'd have to go back to school and study things way over my head."

"If you can build stone structures you can build IT. Learn it anyway."

"Hell, I have dirt under my fingernails, and build fireplaces and stone walls with my hands. I come from a family of masons; build things with brick and stone, sometimes with wood. I like working with stone because that kind of life is part of me. Poppi always talked about making patterns with stone. It's a piece of history, stone lasts a long time."

"You could sell your business to Moses," Sue said. "He takes care of it most of the time now anyway, doesn't he? And the way he talks it sounds like he enjoys it, and I've seen he's got few helpers. I remember hearing you say that you've wanted to do something else, and it's never too late to learn. What about the writing? You still like to do that don't you?"

"I just write for myself, and haven't published anything of any significnace. Really not thinking about doing much writing now. It's hard getting into the writing mode, but never say never." Michael looked up at the ceiling, thoughts rolling in mind, then said, "Sell the business my grandfather started?" then he shook his head. "I just couldn't do that."

"It's just a way to keep it, and leave it," Sue said.

"It doesn't seem right. I'd feel like I was cutting off my own arm. Poppi built the business from nothing, and I know he'd want me to keep it going for as long as feasibly possible. We make money, pays the bills. I'm part of it, the cabin is part of me, and you too."

"The cabin in Hungry Point will always be home to you, won't it?"

"Yes, and that's really our home too," Michael said. "This place is just temporary, right? Don't you think we'll move back there someday? The main reason for coming here was for you to get to know your parents, and for them to get to know you after finding out they were alive."

"And I want to get to know them."

"I was more than glad to move here, so you could be close to them, but you're right my life's in Hungry Point. I'm attached to Hungry Point forever I think, and it'll always be home. I'm here to be with you because it's what I thought you wanted, and I want you to be happy. You should get to know your parents. I wish only for you be happy. I can't imagine if my parents turned up alive after such a long time. I'd freak out. You get to know them, and I'll be here for you."

"You don't mind traveling back and forth from Hungry Point?"

"It's fine, and I'll do it for you as long as it takes, until you say you're ready to move back," Michael said. "You'll be going back to see your step-dad, Kick sometimes. He's always happy as hell to see us, well you, especially. Always smiling when he sees you. Some of our friends we grew up with are still planted around there, everybody knows everybody. Hungry Point is like one big family."

"I like Hungry Point," Sue said, "but you're right, I want to get to know my mom and dad, too. I missed out on a lot of years with them. And they like you. I know they do."

"Yeah, I guess it's just me. Lately things have been moving pretty fast. Let's try to take one day at a time. Want to go out and celebrate? We can tell everybody about the baby tomorrow. Tonight's just for us, so let's celebrate."

"Okay," Sue said. "Let's go to, Reds, the curry place, we haven't been there for a while."

"I fell in love with that place the first time we went there," Michael said.

"The place feels so close to me. We've been going there for years. This town makes me feel the same, like I've lived here for years."

"I remember the first time, and how you looked," Sue said. "I got that feeling from you too. I wonder why?"

Michael leaned over and kissed Sue. "Maybe it's dejavu? Okay, I'll take a quick shower, and will head out for Reds."

"I'll change, and wait for you," she said, and wrapped her arms around Michael hugging him in a bear grip, then their lips collided, seeming to make contact in every way that was utterly possible. Sue looked at Michael. "Okay, take your shower, and we'll head out."

"Not sure I want this moment to ever stop," Michael said.

"It's not stopping," Sue said. "It's just a timeout."

PANIC TIME

After about twenty minutes Michael stepped out of the shower feeling shiny and new, washed and waxed, fresh like morning dew. From the bathroom he yelled, "Ready to go?" but heard no answer from Sue, so he repeated, "Ready to go?" then poked his head through the doorway, and looked left, right, around the room with no sign of Sue. *I wonder where she is? Is she here? Why is it so quiet?*

He finished drying off, got dressed, combed his hair, rubbed in some beard oil from a new batch he'd just bought and mixed through his beard, then went into the kitchen, but she wasn't there.

She's playing games with me, he thought.

"I know you're here, somewhere," he said, and jokingly added in a raised voiced, "I'll find you because I'm pretty good at hide and seek," then he went into the bedroom. "Here I come." The room was quiet enough that he heard his own heart beat, and felt his breath around his face. While breathing in and out he scanned the walls and corners of the room, then focused on the walk-in closet doors.

She must be in there, he thought, and baby-stepped his way in that direction. His hand slowly grabbed, turned the door handle. Then jerking opened the door ready to surprise her, he was surprised to see there were only empty lifeless shirts, sweaters, jackets, and pants swinging back and forth, moving from the coil of air created from opening the door. He swivelled around after he thought he'd felt something from behind, but there was no one in view, and only saw his shadow painted on the wall from the window light.

His next steps were deliberate as he searched the room, then reached for the next closet handle, and with one rapid movement pulled open that door, then stared at the clothes inside, and whispered, "Sue, where the hell are you? What's going on?"

He turned toward the living room and scanned that space, but there wasn't anywhere else to hide because the apartment was a small place. "Where are you?" he said in a lost voice, then looked at the sofa, where he'd heard the news about the baby, where she told him about seeing the doctor and their plans. *The happy sofa*, he thought, and pulled the cushions to the side.

"The ultra-sound picture," he said, looking at it, then in the next moment reaching down, grabbing, and holding it. "Where the hell is she? This is nuts. What's going on? She was just here!"

Holding the ultra-sound picture in his hand, and while looking at it, he looked up at the walls of the apartment, which were blurred, and he became confused. "What's the hell is happening?" Michael seemed to feel dizzy, and blacked out after seeing a vision of flashing images, then his thoughts went deep to another place as his mind traveled through time and space.

The room spun, or felt that way as he rocked back and forth while his arms reached out to grip some support, but there was nothing to grab from where he stood in the middle of the room because everything was out of reach. Collapsing to the floor, landing on his face, Michael rolled on his back. Now he was staring at the ceiling, and watching it open like a curtain at the movies or stage show.

A myriad of images flashed accompanied by a vibrating bell ringing echo that became louder and louder, then softer, then louder, and soft again. His body felt glued to the floor by a force parallel to nothing he'd ever experienced, paralyzed in a silent world, exploring the universe of his mind.

The body he inhabited acted like a conduit holding a river of information, and flowing with knowledge. He was caught and unable to escape, just a prisoner in its wave. The air he inhaled was fuel and energy that changed from slow to quick, heavy to soft, then gentle, and finally to desperate.

He imagined being the pilot of a plane flying through dark clouds and storms trying to maintain control while looking for a safe place to land. Then a runway lit up ahead reflecting a narrow lane and where to put down. Eyes on the instruments he guided the plane down and after rolling slowly, finally came to a stop, and closed his eyes in relief. How much time had passed he didn't know, it could've been ten minutes, an hour, a day, week, a month, a year. But when he opened his eyes, he was back in the room on the floor flat on his back, then after a moment sat up shaking out the nerves.

What the hell was that? He raised his hands, they were numb, so he squeezed his fingers into a fists repeatedly, massaging them until life and feeling returned.

Michael picked up the ultra-sound picture. *Sue,* he thought. *Where's Sue?*
Their apartment was on the second floor of an older three-story Victorian house that had been turned into individual apartments, two downstairs on the first floor, their apartment along with another one on the second floor, and one small faraway small room up dark steep steps on the third floor with only a glimmer of the door at the top of the stairs.

The house was situated at the end of a dead-end road just on the outskirts of town near a wooded area, and the only cars were drivers lost and turning around. From what Michael understood, the old house was owned by a friend of Sue's newly found parents.

Michael knocked on the neighbor's apartment door on his floor, but no one answered, he guessed no one was home. He looked at the dark narrow steep stairs that went up to the third floor, then down to the first floor and decided to check outside.

He walked down to his car that was parked on the street in front where he'd left it. *Where is she?* he thought, and headed for his car. After walking around the car, looking through the windows, he opened the door, and everything was the same as he'd left it. "Where did she go?"

He looked up and down the street, then at the house and saw a figure of someone looking out of the third story window. *Haven't met the people who live in that apartment yet.*

He got into the car checking, thinking, and searching for anything that looked off kilter, then just as he was going to get out of the car and go back into the apartment. Michael blinked, closed and opened his eyes, and at that moment a car pulled up, stopped a little far away on the other side of the street. A man got out, his arms waving in the air above his head, shouting louder than he'd ever heard, GET OUT OF THE CAR! - GET OUT OF THE CAR!

Michael just looked at him, astonished, thinking, *What the hell is he yelling at?* then realized the engine was running.

Again, the man yelled GET OUT! GET OUT! - IT'S ON FIRE! IT'S ON FIRE!

Michael sat stunned as the man ran over, opened the car door, grabbed and tried to drag him out of the car into the street. "Are you okay?" the man asked Michael.

"What are you talking about? What's on fire?"

First he was confused, but now he could see the flames and smoke rising from beneath the front of the car where the engine was located. They ran across the street, and fell in the empty lot opposite the car.

Michael closed his eyes, moaning out of breath, feeling he'd escaped near death.

"Thanks man," Michael said."

"You okay?" the man asked. "What happened to your car? Have you done any work on it recently? It just started on fire! Must be a reason for that happening."

"I don't know," Michael said. "I did have some work done on the engine, and thought it was fine, with no problems." He looked at the window again, but this time there was no one in the window of the third story apartment.

The man pulled Michael to a nearby tree and propped him up. "You stay here. I'll call the fire department. You are one lucky guy."

They watched Michael's car being engulfed in flames. "Hey, man thanks for helping, and getting me out of the car before it blew up. You saved me," Michael mumbled and closed his eyes.

Then after some time he opened them, suddenly he was back in the car, sitting there like nothing had happened as he looked around stunned, overtaken by shock and surprise. "What is this?" he said. "What's going on? There's no one here, and the car's not on fire. Is this a dream? Where's Sue? I've got to figure out what's happening. This is strange, so strange."

He made his way back across the street and to the house. Being that they'd just moved into the apartment, had only met, and just talked to a few people who lived in the place, he thought, *Is this a good idea?* and hesitated to ask anything about Sue. On top of that he really didn't know if anyone was even there or at home.

He had met the neighbor on the first floor, a lady about in her thirties, who worked at a fitness center as a trainer. Her name was Lori. She was Asian, slim, tall, and sinewy with short black hair, and looked like a Tom Boy.

He'd heard there was Latino couple with two kids who were in elementary school in the other downstairs apartment. The dad worked at a garage, running his own business, fixing cars from what he'd heard, and his wife worked part time keeping track of the accounts. They moved from Florida for a change of pace, and at first struck by the difference in temperature, but said they liked the changes in seasons.

A retired couple lived in the apartment next to Michael and Sue on the second floor. From the short time he'd lived there, found they were always up early out doing things together, walking, shopping, playing golf, and always eating out. From the few conversations they'd had together, Michael found out that the old guy was a retired insurance salesman, and his wife freelanced as an accountant for some small businesses clients. The old guy liked telling jokes. One went like this, What do you get when you mix an elephant and a rhinoceros? A hell if I know. Then he'd say that one is always a knee slapper.

Originally meeting through clients they had both worked for discovered they enjoyed each other's company, and got hitched. They looked in pretty good shape for their age, the woman kept her gray hair set, he was bald with a goatee. Every time Michael had seen them, which wasn't that many because he and Sue had just moved to the new place, they were dressed in sporty looking clothes. They liked taking pictures and selfies for social media, so Sue connected with them on social media.

Neither Sue nor Michael had met the tenant on the third floor, and didn't know how many people lived in that aparetment, but occasionally heard footsteps and muffed voices. Michael made his way back into the house, and out of ideas of where to look next, so he decided to go up to the third-floor apartment to introduce himself, but mainly to see if they had heard or knew anything to help find Sue. He traversed up the squeaky steps, slowly, carefully planting his feet, and when he got to the top step of third floor, stopped, and thought, *I wonder if anyone's home.*

He made his way across the floor and knocked on the door. No sound nothing, no answer, but thought he'd heard some movement inside the apartment, so he put his ear to the door, listened, and knocked again.

Someone's definitely moving around in there, he

thought, and stood quietly, waiting. He knocked again, but no one came to the door. As he turned and started to walk down the stairs the door to the apartment squeaked opened. Michael stopped, his head snapped around to see the door had opened revealing a crack of light, and the glimpse of an eye from what looked to be a kid peering at him. Michael raised his hand to wave as the door slammed shut.

"A kid," Michael said, "just a kid at the door." He went back and knocked a few times with no answer, so he decided to head back to his apartment. After walking in he stood in the living room, then his eyes turned up at the ceiling after hearing footsteps from the apartment above.

Should I go back up to try and talk to whoever came to the door, probably pointless?

His stare followed the sound of the footsteps across the ceiling. Then Michael jumped and turned as the apartment door opened, then watched Sue walk in with two bags of groceries in her arms. Michael looked at Sue stunned. "Where did you go? I've been worried, wondering where you were, and where you went. Why didn't you say something, or write a note?"

"I don't know," Sue said. "Just thought I'd get some groceries for the weekend since you were in the shower. I wasn't gone that long. Are you okay?" She put the bags on the table and touched his head.

"You're sweating. Were you exercising? What's wrong? Why are you so jittery?"

"Why didn't you leave a note?"

"I told you I just went to the store to pick up some food," she said.

"Why would I leave a note when I was coming right back? What's wrong? You've never acted like this before. I thought you'd be able to figure out that I'd be right back. Where did you think I went?"

"I was going crazy worrying where you were," he said. "I knocked on the other apartment doors thinking you may be visiting our neighbors."

"I'm sorry," she said. "I didn't think it was such a big deal. What's wrong? You're acting a little strange."

"Have you seen the people who live on the third floor?" he asked.

"No, I haven't," she said. "How are they? Nice?"

"Don't know I've only talked the couple downstairs a few times," he said. "I don't know about the other neighbors, just said hello to everyone, and saw a young kid upstairs on the third floor who only opened the door for a second. He didn't say anything."

"What was the kid like?"

"He slammed the door after I said hello. I just saw his eyes peering through the crack of the door. Kind of creepy. I don't know, couldn't really see anything. It seemed strange, but had a familiar twist, like connected to a memory. I really don't know what to say about it."

"Well, okay, that's that," she said, "and everything's put away. I'm done. You ready to eat?"

Michael stood by the door with a puzzled feeling. "You don't seem concerned about what happened."

"Nothing happened," Sue said. "I went to buy groceries."

"Let's go eat," Michael said.

On the way out to eat they ran into the older couple who lived downstairs.

"How are you folks doing?" the older woman asked.

"We're fine, just going out to eat. I know we've met each other a few times since we moved here, but never properly introduced ourselves. I'm Sue, and this is Michael."

"I'm Fred, Fred Barker, probably told that, and this is my wife, Alice."

They shook hands, and Fred went into his joke routine. "Say have you heard what you call a pig that does karate?" There was a pause waiting for the punch line. "A pork chop. What do you call a fake noodle?" Pause again. "An impasta."

"That's funny," Sue said. "The one joke I always tell is about the dog that went crazy."

"Why did the dog go crazy?" Fred asked.

"Because it's owner named it, Stay."

Fred laughed. "That's a good one. I'm going to steal it."

"Please use it. I think we've talked briefly a couple of times going in or out, and nice to finally really meet. Maybe we can have dinner sometime."

"Dinner sounds good, and I remember we spoke a little the day we moved in," Michael said. "You mentioned you were in insurance, right Fred?"

"Still dabble in it a little, collecting, and selling art," Fred said. "Enjoying life as much as possible. But if you need some insurance I can line you up. We were just in Hawaii last month for two weeks. What's the scariest day in Hawaii?" Pause. "Hula-ween."

"Funny, funny," Sue said. "We went there a couple of years ago. It's a beautiful place. How often do you go there?"

"Once a year," Fred said. "Got a time share. If we don't go we exchange it for another place or just sell the two weeks. It's popular, so there's no problem finding people who want to go to Hawaii. Let me know if you'd like to use it. I'll give you a good deal."

"Sure will think about it. I'd like to go there again. Well, we won't keep you," Michael said. "Nice talking to you again, and we'll see you around sometime. Maybe we can get together for dinner sometime."

"Have a nice evening," Fred said.

"Likewise," Michael said.

"Bye," Sue said.

They got into Michael's car, a restored Ford Mustang that he'd had since high school. "Still want to go to the curry place?"

"Don't you?" Sue asked.

"Yeah, I think it's the easiest place to get a table without waiting to long."

"Curry place then," she said. "Drive on my love."

"Buckle up darling," Michael said, and smoked the tires leaving two black marks trailing behind with the lingering smell of burnt rubber.

"You're crazy," Sue said. "I know it's fun for you, but do you need to do that every time?"

"Got to be crazy sometimes." Michael turned on the radio and found a station playing rock music. "There's that song again. The one you were listening to when I got home."

THE CURRY PLACE

"Not many cars around here today," Michael said. "Probably get busier in a while. Oh well, it's good for us. Hey, look over there a perfect spot just for us to park." Michael easily drove into the parking place without a care. "Well that worked out pretty well. Guess luck's on our side today."

"Luck is on our side, really? It's still early," Sue said. "And you're probably right that'll it gets busier closer to dinner time." Then very soon car after car arrived, and the lot was full. Michael looked at Sue and they both laughed.

"See," Michael said, "look at all of the cars coming. Told you, luck is on our side."

They got out, and took the short walk down a hill toward the restaurant, checking a shops, and other restaurants along the way.

"Been in that shop before," Sue said. "I remember they had some interesting things. That's where I bought a wooden carving of a cobra snake in that shop, and gave it to Kick for his birthday. Snakes are his favorite reptile, and he keeps it behind the bar."

"I've seen it, and ever since I was a kid going there with Poppi, he talked about snakes. Not only does Kick like snakes, he knows a lot about them for some reason."

As they made their way through the door of Reds, Sue said, "Curry smells great, and making me hungry. We made the right choice coming here."

Reds had been in business for some time, was popular with locals, the tourists, and virtually anyone walking nearby would be taken over by the aroma of curry. Tourists who went to visit Hilltop Park usually ate at Reds, and everyone who went to the park saw the sign with the big red letters, and arrow pointing in the direction of the restaurant. There was always a different comment or saying placed on the sign to capture the moment of the experience, and it left an imprint in the mind.

The restaurant was small, had five tables, one chef, and usually only one waitress who changed from time to time depending on the day. The actual owner of Reds would pop in from time to time and talk to the chef, change a picture hanging on the wall, or add some ornament that he'd picked up on one of his travels to dress up the restaurant. Not everything displayed was from India, but all the trinkets he'd picked up made interesting conversational give and take for the customers, and these items made good props in photos for advertising the place.

The walls were painted a peach color, had green trim at the baseboard and ceiling, so if you looked closely you may have been able to see a pattern bureied deep inside. The place was bright with scenic pictures of structures, mountains, and places from around India, Myramar, and Napal, hanging on the wall. On one end there was a small bar with a part of the counter that would lift up, so workers could pass from the kitchen to the main part of the place. A glass fridge cooler that had bottles of different kinds of beer and other drinks on the side. In back and barely visible was the work area and stove. A tandoori oven for open cooking in the traditional way sat near the front or behind the counter; it pulled the tourists over to get a picture giving customers an opportunity to watch how Naan bread, chicken, or other food was cooked.

Michael and Sue walked into the restaurant and waved to the chef who recognized and greeted them with a Hello, and welcome back in a strong Indian brogue.

"Good evening," the waitress said. "For two?"

"Yes," Michael said, "just us."

She showed them to a table near the counter. "Here are your menus," she said. "Would you care for something to drink?"

"Yes, I'll have a beer," Michael said, "How about a Kingfisher."

"Make it two, Sue said," raising her her hand while holding up two fingers.

After bringing the drinks the waitress had what seemed like a long conversation with other customers, greeting, asking if they'd been to Reds before, describing the food on the menu, and finally agreeing what was to be ordered. A half business deal, home cooked meal feeling.

The waitress made it back to Michael and Sue's table and took their order. "Okay, very good," the waitress said, and went to the kitchen showing it to the chef. There was some nodding, questions, pointing, and ended with the order attached in clip above the the stove where the chef could see it and cook.

"I don't think this place has changed much since we were last here," Michael said. "Guess that's why I like it because it feels like home."

"Only the servers' change," Sue said. "Pretty sure it was a different person the last time we were here. Do you recall how we found this place?"

"Kick brought us here," Michael said. "It was on your birthday."

"You remember," Sue said. "and of course I had a great time that night. I remember we were singing songs all night."

"I had a great time, too, still have good memories," Michael said, then smiled and held up his beer. "Drank a little too much of this stuff that night though, but there's no forgetting that night, especially after getting home." He winked knowing Sue remembered as well.

"So, you were worried today when you couldn't find me today," Sue said. "Running around looking and checking where I was. That was pretty crazy."

"I don't know what came over me," Michael said. "I had a strange feeling, maybe because we'd just moved into the place. I think I passed out for a few minutes. I don't know. Now I'm going to worry even more about you with a kid coming."

"Are you okay, Michael? I was really worried about you today after that happened."

"Yeah, everything's going to be fine," Michael said.

"Don't fret," Sue said. "People move and have kids every day. It seems normal to feel some anxiety and stress."

"I know, I know," Michael rattled on, then held up his glass. "Here's to our new addition." They raised and clinked them together. "I like the sound of that.

"To our new boy or girl!" Sue said, and drank her beer.

The waitress came over to their table with the food. "Enjoy your meal?"

"Thanks, it looks fantastic."

As they began to eat, two obviously drunk men walked into the restaurant, and sat at a smaller table at the other end of the restaurant near window facing the street. They were both tall, stocky, had well trimmed beards, short slicked back dark hair. They wore suits like business men, but their look didn't fit the picture of businessmen, and were more like football players. They were noisy, spoke in loud voices, babbling on problems with collegues and work, so everyone could overhear what they were saying. But basically their conversation was about the last bar they'd been at, and the first time they'd been to it, so they were from parts unknown.

"I think we've been to the bar they're talking about," Michael said.

"Fantastic," Sue said in a nonchalant way. "Who cares? Does it matter?"

"Want to go there later?" Michael asked.

"No, not tonight," Sue said, "don't really feel like it, but will if you want to go. I game to tag along."

"No, we can just go home," Michael said. "You've had a busy day, finishing the unpacking, doctor, and the news about the baby. It's a lot to take in, so let's just head home."

"I'm fine," Sue said. "We can do anything you like."

"Okay," Michael said. "Let's think on it, and decide

after we finish eating."

The two guys continued talking, eating, drinking, a few more people came into the restaurant, and a few left. Michael and Sue finished their meal, paid, said goodbye to the owner like always, complimenting him on a delicious meal, and told him they'd be back.

PLACES OF INTEREST

Places everywhere hold interest for some rhyme or reason, personal, historical, could be the result of an important event that occurred at that particular place at some time that creates change and memories. Significant events become historical for people to read and talk about, and use poetic license to exaggerate for excitement and thrills.

If you think about controversial or life changing, times, which ones come to mind? Probably for most people it's basically a trip, especially a long one. Could be a wedding, when children are born, family or a close friend die, a war, famous person is assassinated. And your choices of what you consider a milestone may depend on the country you're from or currently live.

Landing on the moon was a worldwide event, but some people believe it was a hoax because for the time in question there's talk that technology and computers were not capable to handle the calculations needed for such an endeavor. Why aren't people working and living on the moon now?

So if some believe that was a hoax, then what other events were actually made up or planned for dubious reasons. Is history written by an unknown entity, powerful people, by winners of war? After time passes a lot of human details are forgotten, and even with all of the visual evidence available for all to see, people still forget things even from the recent past.

He remember being in Hawaii years ago staying at a condo he rented. One night after dinner listening to the radio while driving back from a restaurant, He skipped through stations trying to find some good music. Then heard the radio host of one station talking about Princess Diana, and found it odd how the radio person was talking about the event, and wondered why they were using the past tense to describe her, and some things about her life. Then as he listened more, discovered she had been killed in a car accident in France. The details were sketchy up to that point, they were talking about her life, and how it had changed after becoming a princess, but there was no doubt that she had died. A scandal would incubate, and differerent sides would make there argument for what had happened.

In some of his dreams certain personal events he would never forget, or how and when they happened as a young child, in high school at sixteen years of age or later in life. The events were the same, only the time and sequence would be different. It was strange that Michael had experienced these same events at different ages in his life. Many other memories were also repeated at different points of time, the events always turned out the same in the end, but again and again the time and place of its happening changed.

The dreams he would have continued in sequence changing day by day, night by night, but in the end the result was always the same, and usually he recalled only bits and pieces. In one dream a friend of a friend borrowed his older brother's car while cruising Main Street, Michael was asked if he wanted to go for a ride. He agreed, and sat in the back seat, then for a time they cruised the streets of the glowing lit town. Michael spotted another good friend during this time, so they stopped and picked him up. Finally they decided to drive over the hill of another valley to a nearby town and grab a pizza.

On the drive back Michael had fallen asleep in the back seat, and only remembered waking up when the car began rolling down a hill after taking a sharp corner. When the car came to a stop upside down, he heard the voices of his friends shouting if everyone was okay. All passengers in the car replied they were okay, save one, the guy Michael had asked to come along for a ride. Climbing out of upside down car they discovered him pinned beneath the car, his legs protruding from under the frame. They called his name, he didn't reply, and thought the worst, that he had been killed. After making a conclusion as that, it seems hard to have joy in your life especially after such an event, and bearing that sort of responsibility. Michael had asked him to ride along, and he thought about dying, and knew it could come at any unknown time. For some reason we think it always will happen to someone else.

Everyone has their own list of events and prioritize them according to importance, the outcome, and finally how they relate. Then add and remember the personal times and places that we all possibly may or may not have experienced, but without exception the two milestones familiar to all people, and those are birth and death.

Birth is not remembered only observed by others, and recorded for family and friends, and we can't tell anyone about death, at least after the fact. But what if we could remember the day when we're born, and tell people about what happens at and after death? I can't think of anyone remembering the experience and knowing their own birth, but observation of death, that experience, that moment, I know all witness, unless their death happens during sleep. This birth and death milestone is related to writings in the Bible, especially in the case of how after Christ died on the cross, rose three days later, and returned to tell the apostles about being reborn.

Whether it's engraved in stone, written on paper, seen on TV, or observed online, there are events that take place daily the same way over and in dreams. These stories flow through life, stories on the the web at real time. Some we can't verify, but they still spread, die or grow into a life of their own depending on how we feel and how others feel. He can tell people where he was born; they'll probably believe him but what if he's not telling the truth? How would they know if there's no evidence to back up what he's been telling them. He actually was only sharing information about what he had been told throughout time. If this can happen so easily, how easy would it be for the more important events we hear about from all over the world to be skewed? What's really true and what's not? People believe what they want to believe, and feel it's really that simple, especially when time is added to the equation.

The first real memory Michael recalled was falling down a hill when as a young boy after skirting a tree that was blocking the path to the road. That particular moment played over and over in his memeory. There was an image of a circular path worn around a tree as it was frequently traveled. And he would think it was his first memory, but had some doubt on occasion and wasn't sure what happened after that.

There were dreams from the past occasionally, but the people in them were out of place and from another time. Are they from that time as well? Nothing was certain, out of bounds, or off limits, and when it came to thoughts and machinations of the mind, because nothing is really certain.

The easiest way to find a starting point is to talk about where you are now, and work your way back while at the same time we know we're moving forward. At the moment Michael is in another country, and it's far from where he grew up. He doesn't remember being born, but has evidence of where that event happened, an old passport with a black and white baby picture glued on the first page showing that he was born in Salzburg, Austria. He's not alone in this, after all, he thought many people are born in one country, and have grown up in another.

Another clear memory is being near a river, The Mississippi River, where he lived ten minutes away, fished, camped, hiked, and walked along it watching the flow of water south.

The memory of moving there is vague, but there was a nice house with a garage, a big vegetable garden, and it sat near a small IGA grocery store that sold delicious ice cream. He remember the big red letters on the front of the store. He fished every weekend, then cleaned and grilled the fish after. He also remember watching some men building homes or some types of structures.

After that he couldn't remember, there were gaps, and the memories were blank or cloudy, but some of another place come to mind, one strong memory is a very big old three story brick house. Something happened at that house, and the old wooden door on the third floor was unforgettable.

A WALK IN THE PARK

They stopped in front after leaving and closing the restaurant door, then stood silent a moment taking in the evening air, watching people walking under the lights. They stood on a street glowing with reflections bouncing off storefront windows under a blanket of stars.

"Man, I'm full, my stomach feels like exploding," Michael said.

"Food's always so good at this place, and that guy who cooks sure is easy going. He always looks so excited and friendly, and gives off the feeling he really likes what he does, makes cooking seem easy for him."

"That's the way life should be," Sue said. "People are

like that when they enjoy their work. Everyone should try to find something they really like doing. No one should spend their life doing something they despise or just do for the money, unless they're doing it to learn. What's his name?"
"I think they call him Bunny."

"Why that name?"

"It's not that he has big ears, maybe because he never stops talking, cooking or preparing food, organizes everything like a conductor at a symphony hall. Nicknames, who knows why people have or they get them, no one does." Then Michael began to remember nicknames of people. Punky, Spratt, Snake, Bootsy, Big-T, TJ, Lanky, images went by so fast that he couldn't make out any of the faces, then it stopped.

"Hello," Sue watched Michael. "Are you okay?"

Michael shook his head. "Fine, fine, say, remember that park we've gone to near here?" Michael said.

"Which one?"

"You know the one that has the running path, and the long arched canopy tunnel of trees. It's just a few minutes from here. We been there a few times running and walking around. Last time we were here to eat we took a walk through there."

"You want to go there now?" Sue asked. "Why? You feel like running?"

"Not to run," Michael said, "just a jaunt around one time. We could make it a tradition when we come to eat here. Let's just go for a walk, talk about our future, and how it'll be raising a kid. It's not too far, and a nice walk. It'll be good."

"Okay, sure, why not," Sue said. "Some good exercise to burn off the calories we've added from dinner. Can't hurt to go for a little walk. You lead the way."

Michael grabbed, and held Sue's hand. They walked at a steady clip remembering and talking the other times they'd been there, smiling, looking at each other, seemingly they could read each other's mind.

"There's the entrance. How many times should we go around? Only once, twice?"

"Oh, yeah, I'm good for a walk, two times around," Sue said.

"I can do that, and shouldn't take too long. Are you sure you're up for it?"

"Are you? If I remember there are a few different ways we can go, the easy way or the hard way."

"Sounds like a challenge," Michael said. "Let's see what you can do?"

They walked up the hill to where the path split into two trails, and veered toward the one on the right going up some stone steps covered over by the canopy of trees, leaves, and branches. Seeing it now was just the way Michael had talked about and remembered when they left the restaurant. The street lights above them had just turned on and reflected through the branches, while a gentle breeze juggled the leaves dropping a few to the ground creating moving shadow patterns around their feet.

"It's such a beautiful night," Sue said. "I get a warm homey kind of feeling being here, like I've been here before."

"Couldn't have said it better myself," Michael said. "And it's beautiful for more than that, one reason, I'm with you. Wow, things are sure going to change this year."

"Are you getting worried?" Sue asked. She took Michael's hand in hers, and squeezed tightly. "We'll be so busy."

"Yeah, a think you're right about that," Michael said. "Having kids is a big step. It hasn't really sunk into my brain yet, but little by little I'm getting used to it, and I know everything will turn out fine."

"You're right things should be fine," Sue said. "And it's normal to be anxious and excited knowing we're going to have a child to take care of. We'll have to come up with a name, and there will be so much else to do. I wonder how things will be in twenty years."

"In twenty years things will really be different, and we'll be holding our grandchildren. Back to things now, I'm sure your newly found parents will want to pitch in," Michael said. "I think we'll have plenty of help."

"They'll probably offer," Sue said, "because this is their first grandchild for my newly found parents and grandparents."

"Okay, I'll call them your parents. Can you tell your dad to stop asking me if I want a job at his company? I really don't want to have that conversation again. The guy offers me a job every time I see him, and still have no idea what the company does, just that it's some kind of IT computer business. He explains things so vaguely, and I'm not a computer person. I have my construction business, busy laying stone, and we're doing okay, don't need their money."

"We'll do whatever you want," Sue said, "and they just want us to know they're here for us if we need them."

"So, when are we telling them?" Michael asked.

"We can call them tonight after we get home," Sue said. "I'm just getting to know them myself, so it's all been a shock for me finding out I have parents after thinking they were gone all this time. Sometimes I think it's all a dream and I'll wake up and be back in Hungry Point."

"I guess we should tell them about the baby right away," Michael said.

"If we don't they'll wonder why nothing was said sooner. They might think I had something to do with keeping it from them; they seem paranoid, well not really paranoid, but strange nonetheless."

"It's getting late," Sue said, "too late to call tonight, so I'll call them tomorrow."

As they walked up the stone steps leading to the park Michael heard some kind of ringing noise, a sound coming from somewhere behind, then in front, but not a sound from nature. Finally it was more like the sound of stones grinding against each other in the vast emptiness of the universe. Images wobbled and flashed in his mind until he closed his eyes as to reset time.

Sue noticed Michael side stepping, wobbling, then he stood still. "You okay," she asked.

"What?" Michael said, then looked around weirdly, he was in a different world, and his eyes rolled backward as he seemed to float.

"You looked lost in thought there," Sue said. "Where did you go? You alright?"

He turned and looked at Sue with a misplaced stare. "Maybe too much excitement, along with to much food and beer," Michael said.

"I'm fine now, just fine."
Then there were voices in the distance behind them getting louder.

"It sounds like those guys from the restaurant are behind us," Sue said. "Do you think they're following us?"

"The drunken guys from the restaurant?" Michael asked. "Why would they be? Probably just seems that way, and they just wanted to go for a walk to get some fresh air. Can't see why they'd want us for anything unless they're thinking about stealing out stuff. If you're concerned how about walking faster or changing paths just to see how they react."

"Let's turn down that trail over there," Sue said. "I remember it from the last time we were here, and it leads back down to the street and to the restaurant. It's an easy trail to walk."

"Okay," Michael said, "let's go that way, and see if they go the same way." They turned right on the trail walking down the steps, picking up the pace, double timing.

"Well," Sue said, "don't hear anything anymore."

"Maybe I'm just paranoid, but been feeling that way since I went looking for you after I came out of the shower. Let's go over there, and watch from behind those rocks. They shouldn't be able to see anything if they walk down this path." There was a trail where others had walked, a little steep, but they were able find a good spot to see where they'd just walked, and could observe everyone coming down the path. "I don't hear voices anymore," Michael whispered.

"I don't either," Sue said, then smiled, but as she caressed Michael's face his eyes rolled back, closed, and he fell to his knees, then prone on his stomach. Turning on his back she watched his body shake and vibrate on the ground. "Michael, are you okay? Michael?" Sue froze, and not knowing what to do watched him, then knelt down next to Michael with her hands raised, squeezed them into fists, almost in tears.

"Michael, Michael!"

He grabbed her hand, squeezed it tight grip, holding on for dear life as if he were falling, then as a breeze floated through, Michael opened his eyes and looked at Sue. "Hi!" he said in a calm voice.

"Should I call an ambulance?" she asked.

"What," he said dazed, and clearly no idea of what had just happened "You were out a few minutes. Just out, and I was freaking out!"

"No, no, I'm fine," he said, and sat up shaking his head. "We don't have to worry about those guys anymore, they're gone."

"I didn't think we had to worry about them at all in the first place," she said. "And what do you mean gone?"

"Gone," he said. "They've left, and won't be back, let's go home."

MEMORIES RETURN

They got into the car, and Michael's first motion as he held the keys in his hand was to start the engine, but he sat silently behind the steering wheel with his fingers gripping it, squeezing tightly, opening and closing his eyes, breathing slowly.

His face was painted deep in thought with an out of this world look. Almost as if he were communicating with someone in another faraway location telepathically, and moaning like having gone through a traumatic life changing experience. A few times it came across as if he would snap out of the blank look he was locked in, but he didn't, and stared straight ahead. His eyes began to glaze over; he was in a trance and touching another world.

Sue hovered over him watching his muscles stretching and twitching, then she nervously asked, "Michael? Are you okay? Are you sure you can drive? I don't like how you look." Sue raised and stretched out her hand, then touched his shoulder, and repeated, "Michael, are you okay?"

He didn't answer, but after giving him a shove, Michael jerked back, his muscles and body became stiff. Then as if electricity from a defibrillator had shocked him back into the present, he became wide eyed, alert, but was silent and just there showing no emotion.

After a moment he turned, then looked at her with an aimless empty expression."What is going on? Where am I?" he said. He was seemingly clueless about what had just happened, and proceeded to wipe and rub his eyes as if he had woken from a deep sleep. "That was weird because I don't know what happened, just blacked out. Sorry, I think I'm okay," he mumbled. "I guess I'm fine, but maybe you should drive, and I'll rest a bit more. I feel a little strange."

"Okay," Sue said, "good idea. Let me drive." Sue got out, and as they changed places she said, "Maybe you should see a doctor? You don't seem to be yourself. You're beginning to act a little different from your normal self, and it seems to have started after we moved, so I could live nearby and get to know my parents better."

Michael looked at her and smiled. "You're having the baby, not me. I don't think I need to see a doctor. I'll be okay, just need some rest. It's been pretty crazy the past few months."

"I don't know, I'm worried about you," she said. "I can't remember anything like this ever happening; never seen you like this before. When was the last time you had a check-up?"

"Check-up?" he said. "I don't remember, but it's been a while, probably the last time I did the doctor thing was in elementary school. Remember when they did those random check-ups occasionally in grade school; you know the check for cavities. We'd chewed on those red tablets."

"My teeth were all red," Sue said. "What was in those red tablets they gave us? It was to show where cavities might form?"

"Mine were all red too after chewing them. Everyone thought it was some kind of a joke." Michael leaned over and kissed Sue on the cheek. "Don't worry . . . I'm fine now, and I'll be okay."

"This is different from checking for cavities. When did you start feeling like this?" Sue asked. "I think it was after I found out about my parents being alive, soon after we went to eat with them. Do you think it's connected to that?"

"Well, your newly found dad pummeled me with questions the whole time, maybe that triggered something. But really, I don't know why these episodes, or whatever they're called started, but I'm pretty sure it has nothing to do with my health, almost one-hundred percent sure of that. I think you're right about when it started though, about that time, I mean. You know I'm seeing flashes of things, reoccurring memories, and reliving bits and pieces of what I did in the past. Some of these episodes involve people I feel I know for some reason, just can't match the faces together with the events, and some aren't connected to anything I've done or know at all."

"You sound certain that it has nothing to do with your health, but I'm not so sure," she said. "We all have memories that trouble us, but usually don't go through what you are now. I know I keep saying this, but I've never seen you like this. I think you should have a check-up just to put yourself at ease. Go get checked out, I did. I need you in tip-top condition to help me when the baby comes. I can't do it all on my own because there will be too much for one person to do."

"Okay, I'll get a check-up," he said, "but no use worrying about now because I can't get one tonight, so for now lets just forget it, and just go home." Michael sat back, closed his eyes, and dozed off. As Sue drove his attention span was in and out now and again, and he didn't say much on the way back, only mumbling in agreement with Sue about the coming future raising a kid in what they both to be an unstable world.

Sue turned on the radio, and while tuning landed on an easy rock station playing some Bob Dylan songs. The music played as Sue drove back to the house as she kept an eye on the traffic and Michael. *This has been happening more and more recently*, she thought. *Why?*

Back at the apartment Sue parked the car, and watched Michael a few minutes as he slept, and mumbled still in some kind of trance. She listened to him breath, and thought, *He'll be okay*, then touched his head.

"What's going on?" he blurted. Jarred and surprised he jerked forward, grabbed her arm, sat up, and squeezed tightly.

She looked down at her arm and how he held it. "Pretty tight grip there," Sue said, and first shook off his hand, then took his hand in hers, smiled, and said it's okay. We're home now Prince Charming, and it's time to wake up. You were really out," she said, "slept the whole time. Still having the same dreams?" She watched him stretch his arms as he woke up, a smile appeared. "You look happy," Sue said. "Have a nice dream?"

"Yeah, I was dreaming about Poppi, and some of the bedtime stories he told me when I was a kid. Was I out a long time?"

"Pretty much the whole trip back," Sue said, "just some snoring."

"I snore?"

"Yes, you don't believe, you do? Really, that's what you think. I'm recording you someday, so you can hear for yourself. You snore like a freight train rolling down railroad tracks."

"I guess a little rest is all I needed because I feel great now. I feel like I slept all night, or just got back from a great vacation. Want to go out again? It's still early enough to get a drink."

"What? Go out again?" she said. "No, I don't want to go out again because we just got back. We're going up to the apartment and rest. Both of us need to rest, and I especially need it after what's been happening with you. You sure have changed your tone and attitude from the short time you were asleep. I was awake watching you, and it wasn't fun for me."

"I feel so good, actually amazing," he said, "but you're right. Let's just go up and take it easy."

"I can make you something to eat if you're hungry," Sue said. "And we have some leftovers in fridge from last night."

"I'm not really hungry, but that could change," he said. "Do we have any beer?"

"We've always got beer," she said.

"Then we're in good shape. What more could a guy ask for? Let's make some popcorn and watch a movie." As they walked up the stairs to their apartment Michael said, "I hear the phone ringing?"

"Yeah, sounds like it," Sue said just as she put the key in the lock.

They walked into the apartment, and Michael picked up the phone. "Hello," he said, but no one was at the other end of the line. "Hello, anybody there?" he put the phone down wondering who had called.

"Who was it," Sue asked, "for me, or for you?"
"I don't really know," he said. "Someone was there, I think, but they didn't say a word, and just cut the call after I answered."

"Doesn't it show the number of the caller?"

"Yeah, there's a number, but I don't recognize it. In fact, don't think I've ever seen it before, and no name."

"Try calling back, if you're curious," she said.

"Won't they call back if they want to?" he said. "Probably not important, just selling something."

Sue stood in front of the open fridge. "There's some leftover pizza, fried potatoes, and salad. I'll warm it up while you sit and relax." She walked into the living room with a beer in hand. "Here, for you. Sit back, relax, and I'll bring you something to eat."

"Let's make some popcorn after, and watch a movie?" Michael said

"Which one?"

"How about this one," Michael said. "It's good, and I like Marlon Brando. Haven't seen it in a while. I'll get it setup."

"A gangster movie?" Sue said. "Okay, if you like."

"Not just a gangster movie, it's the greatest gangster movie ever made. And more than just a gangster movie, it's about family and life. "

"I'll make the popcorn," Sue said.

The movie started and Michael watched as the

Godfather listened to a man who was sitting in a chair in front of a desk talk about his family, and how he needed help. *I need help*, he thought. *Who can I call? I wish Poppi were still alive. Maybe Moses can help me figure out what's going on with me.*

TRAINING ASSIGNMENT

Michael became alert, awake, and aware of being in a place lined up with a bunch of guys in a big open room, and got the impression of being in some sort of old government building. A government place because as he looked up saw high ceilings above, and there was a familiar aroma that he seemed to recognize. There were gray metal desks and shelves around the space, and when he looked down saw his bare feet on a worn wooden floor, then wiggled his toes to make sure he was really there, and not just having a dream.

The walls were peeling chipped light gray plaster, and there were old painted wooden case windows, some which had blinds drawn and others that were open.

He, like the other guys standing there, wore only underwear while sunlight bounced in and reflected around the room. His stomach growled and he felt hungry, then noticed a clock on the wall closing in on twelve. *Noon?* he thought, *Where am I?* And while looking around gathering more information figuring out what kind of place he had landed in, then it dawned on him that it was a Army medical checking place.

Am I joining the Army? How old am I? This is not the first time I've been here. I've seen or done this before.

There were two guys in white coats, one stood in front. "Shorts down," the man in front said, then felt Michael's testicles checking for an indication of any sort of problems, and did the same to the other men down the line.

The other guy went behind with a small flashlight. "Bend over and grab your ankles." After going down the line checking everyone's rectum for hemorrhoids, the man ordered all of them to pull up their shorts, then after finishing with some active physical stretching and balance tests they all got dressed.

Next they were let off for lunch to a cafeteria which alson had a familiar aroma. At the end of the counter was a stack of metal trays where they all lined up to get their food and drinks. Then after eating they were back for psychiatric interviews and more tests. When finished they were driven off to a hotel where Michael shared a room with a guy who talked about conspiracy theories. After doing more tests the next day he went home, and waited to hear when he would get orders for boot camp. He knew that the training would be at Fort Polk in Louisiana, but not sure when it would start.

During the bus ride home he thought about the conversation he'd have with Sue. It would be on a sunny day walking on a trail toward the river talking about what the future held, gripping each other's hand knowing they would be apart.

"Are you sure this is a good idea," Sue asked. "It's kind of a surprise because I thought you want to be a builder like your grandfather, making things with stone." "Seems like the right thing to do for now," Michael said. "Poppi was in the service. He's told me stories about it, and how it changed his life, and about the people he's met. I almost feel obligated to go."

"I guess it's good learning discipline, having a physical and knowing you're healthy, but I don't know why you decided to do this so suddenly. You never said anything about it before, just went off without saying a word."

"I'm sorry, it was a spur of the moment thing, and that check was pretty thorough. I won't go onto any details, but a pretty comprehensive physical, they checked in all of the nooks and crannies"

"You won't be able to go fishing after you're sent to an assignment."

"You're right, but most of the training will be outside, and food should be pretty good. Poppi did say it was tough, but believe I'll learn things in a different way whether that's good or bad, I don't know. Sometimes it's good to see things from a different perspective."

"Really," Sue said, "good Army food? It can't compare to what you eat now."

"I'll have a big meal, fill up before leaving, and have a going away party. You'll come won't you? I need you to be there."

"When are you leaving?"

"In two weeks on a Monday," Michael said. "I just found out. It'll go by fast. I'll finish training, and be back before you know it. That's how time seems to work, just goes by and it's the future before you know it"

"Let's spend as much time together," Sue said. "I'll go to the airport with you to see you off."
"Poppi's been telling me what to expect," Michael said. "He went through basic training years ago, but I'm guessing it probably hasn't changed much, except for the equipment. I have a feeling of what to expect."

They stopped at the bank of the river watching it flow, waving at boats going by, then gathered some driftwood to start a fire. Michael and Sue stayed at the riverside watching the sun set reflect on waves, listening to the evening sounds echo in the air. It was getting dark when they walked back to the cabin.

"When I get back we'll have to celebrate," Michael said. "Let's go camping on the river."

"I'd like that, and you can tell me all about your training adventure."

***

The flight to the military training facility in Louisiana was not in anyway unusual, just a blur and pleasant at the same time, but soon that would all change for all of the new recruits. After arriving on the base Drill Sergeants yelled at the recruits to get off the bus and line up.

"Move it, Move it, get in line."

Michael stood next to a guy he had met during the physical and testing time. "Hey, how are you doing? Is this what you thought and expected it would be like?"

"No, it's pretty crazy, man. Never been ordered around like this before."

"No talking, eyes front," the Sergeant said. "First, everyone will follow me to pick up uniforms, and the gear you'll need, then we'll go to the barracks to clean. We don't want you living in a pigpen, so we'll get it all nice and cozy for you. Now I know you are new to this, and don't know many of the commands, but I presume you all understand English, so let's try doing some marching. Attention! Right face! Forward . . . march! Left, left, go left right left. Go left, go left, go left right left. A yellow bird . . . with a yellow bill . . . landed on . . . my window sill. I lured it in . . . with crubs of bread . . . then I kissed it . . . on the head."

Why have I been dropped into a place not knowing why? This is hard to follow. What am I doing here?

They entered a warehouse filled with uniforms and shoes, going to and from each station, getting the right size uniforms, trying on, and taking two pair of shoes. From there onto the barracks with a fifty pound duffel bag filled with clothes on everyone's shoulder filled with all the gear for the thirteen weeks of training, and future life in the Army.

The barracks was wide open, dull white walls, brown vinyl floor, windows all around, and enough bunks for fifty people lined up on either side of the room. It looked clean except for clumps of dust floating and moving from whiffs of air from movement.

"Line up in front of a bunk," the sergeant said, "toss your duffel on it, and stand at attention." The Drill Instructor walked through the barracks slowly looking at everyone. "This is going to your home for the foreseeable future. Now the first thing we have to do is clean our home. Right?"

"Sir, yes sir," everyone said in a loud agreeing tone.

"I didn't hear you," the sergeant said. "Sound off."

"Sir, yes sir!" everyone yelled, louder.

The Drill Instructor looked around. "Well what are you waiting for?"

A lone unknown voice echoed, "We don't have any tools, supplies, or rags to clean."

The Drill Instructor walked through the middle of the barracks, hands cupped behind his back, with a gazing panning stare. "You've got two hands. Those are all the tools you need today. Get on your knees, and clean the floor with your hands. That's all we have to work with for now. We might get some cleaning supplies if you do a good job. First you people have got to prove to me that you deserve to have supplies."

The rest of the afternoon was spent gathering dust with bare hands, and scraping up piles of lint and dirt until the D.I. was satisfied. After the inspection we marched over to another warehouse style building to get sheets and blankets, then spent the late afternoon learning how to make a bunk and store our things. In front of each bunk was a foot locker to be used for shoes, socks, polish, personal things, and next to each bunk was a tall gray metal locker with a couple of shelves and place to hang uniforms. Lights were out at exactly at 22:00, they slept soundly after a hard first day, and the morning call was at 05:00.

The routine after the morning run: go to the mess hall for breakfast, barracks cleaning, studying, lunch, more training, dinner, cleaning again, and lights out again. That routine stayed the same with a a few changes of learning about weapons, fire guard duty, marching, and occasional visit to the PX.

After basic Michael had a two week break, and instead of going home he decided to stay in a nearby town. After that he started AIT for MOS 25V his job would be creating visual images, audio recording of training, public affairs, occasionally covering combat operations and missions.

Since the military budget was large his division had access to the latest equipment. On the last day he received orders, and would be transferring to Germany after a thirty day leave. He put the envelope with the orders down on the bunk, stretched out, and closed his eyes.

MIND TRAVEL

Stories read in books, magazines, newspapers, and movies are organized with a beginning middle and end. So when we read a story or watch a movie we can follow along to find out or guess what will happen next. Dreams on the other hand are random surprisingly unknown and usually mostly forgotten. Dreams seemly change without any thought, direction, order, or control.

This is completely different when people go on a trip or think about the future. Plans are made and followed to some degree either carefully or badly, and most in most cases with a high degree of success. A spur of the moment change could make for an incredible surprising or awkward ending. And without a doubt when we dream there's always a surprise, for some mysterious reason the outcome is mostly forgotten, but there are exceptions and times when we retain a few scattered parts and pieces of a dream.

So why do we forget most of them and only remember a few bits and pieces? Now that's a good question? Maybe you're dreaming now and perhaps not reading this story? Maybe I'm dreaming now and not writing this story.

So, as soon as we both wake up, everything you've read, and I've written will disappear. We'll wake up in a completely alternative dimension with new a family, and different friends, wondering how we got to where we are as we live through a crazy Rip Van Winkle moment.

***

Michael tossed in bed a little half asleep, half awake, he moved and rolled around changing positions over and over feeling awkward and edgy. Sue woke a few times during the night watching and hearing Michael make indistinct unclear sounds, saying strange words from an incomprehensible foreign language completely unknown to anything known, leaving her wondering if it was a language at all.

After that episode she couldn't sleep and decided to go into the kitchen. While she meandered on her way through the apartment thought, *Things seem to be going to a strange place.* Then standing frozen at the open door of the fridge a moment looking straight ahead into the light she wondered, *Why am I here?* then nodded clearing her mind and grabbed a lemon water. After she moved over beside the table, looked out of the window at a moon glowing in the darkness, then went back to the fridge to search for something to eat.

She took out the bowl of chili made the previous day, scooped out a good amount, and turned on the stove. The aroma from the chili drifted through the apartment and into the bedroom, triggering Michael to wake. He sat up when the chili aroma floating in the air trickled up his nose.

That smells good, he thought while rubbing the sleep from his eyes. *I'm getting me some of that.* Then he made his way down the hall and stood in the doorway of the kitchen watching Sue stir the chili. She was using a big wooden spoon that was part of a set of wooden utensils they'd bought on a trip to Hawaii on a visit to Hawaiian Plantation Village. It was an amazing place that had old homes of different cultures who had brought their life and families along, and for a time lived as they did in their home country.

Michael stood in the doorway to the kitchen. "Hey beautiful, that chili smells good. Too good to let any go to waste. Any left for me?" Sue was wearing a white shirt, and as she turned showed her profile, making him smile after seeing the shirt was unbuttoned at the top. "I remember when you bought that shirt. It still looks great on you, or you look great in it."

"Pull up a chair," she said, "and I'll dish up a bowl for you if you want."

His eyes zeroed in on her Snoopy underwear. "Nothing I'd like better, it smells great! I can't resist," he said, and sat down watching Sue fill his bowl. "You don't usually get up in the middle of the night. Why are you up so early? What's happening today?"

"I was watching you tossing and listening to you talk in your sleep."

"What did I say?"

"Well, that's basically the reason for me waking up, and not being able to go back to sleep. I couldn't understand a word, was just gibberish, all nonsense, bla, bla, bla, stuff."

"What did I say?"

"I told you, it was a strange foreign language I'd never heard before. Almost just like you were mumbling like a person speaking in tongues making up sounds. As far as I know I've never heard you sound like that, or say anything like that. Sorry, to freak you out, but it was weird. I should've recorded you. If it happens again, I'll try and record you."

"Go ahead," he said, "please do that. I like to hear it too because I don't remember saying anything. So, what's the plan for today?"

"I'm meeting my parents for lunch," Sue said. "You're welcome to join us if you like. How about it? Come along?"

"I'm driving back Hungry Point today to help Moses with a job, be gone a couple of days, it's a big project. We can set up a lunch or dinner with your parents another time. Are you going to tell them about our new addition to the family?"

"Of course, that's why I thought it would nice if you were there."

"I'm sorry, but . . . I promised Moses I'd help him, so he's expecting me to show up. It's a job that needs at least two people, maybe a few more."

"It's okay, don't worry, I understand" Sue said. "We'll do something with them another time."

"This chili is really delicious," Michael said. "Did I make this batch?"

"No, I made this batch. Do you want a little more?"

"I'm fine," he said, "this enough. Where are you going for lunch with your parents?"

"I don't know; they made the arrangements. I'm meeting them at their house."

"Their house is quite the place. I noticed the really nice stone work the first time we were there. Well done by an expert craftsman. I wonder who they hired to build it."

"If you come with me you can ask about it? I'm sure they'd be happy to tell you."

"Next time," Michael said. "I'll wash the dishes later, let's go back to bed, and start the morning with a little fun."

A TRIP TO REMEMBER

With a feeling of floating free in an unknown time, and not knowing where he actually was while feeling surrounded by uncertainty, Michael opened his eyes. A moment later he turned toward a brilliant light where he saw a row of small framed windows, and beyond them full white clouds decorating a blue sky.

What is this? Where am I? What is happening?

There was a hum, a sound of engines, and the roar of air whistling over fan blades made the the air tingle. He wondered, *How do I know this?* Then he heard an unfamiliar man's voice. "How's the little fellow doing? Is everything okay? How are you doing? Need anything?"

"We're fine," a woman said. "He's just waking up and probably hungry.

Who is she? And who is she talking to? Who's hungry? Where am I? Why can't I speak?

"He's been sleeping most of the flight," then the woman said. "It's his first time on a plane, but I think he likes flying. Seems to like it anyway up to now, but he's probably too young to remember anything. I'm sure it'll all be a buried memory that he'll wonder about someday, maybe feel something, and think about it when he flys. I've been taking pictures, writing a bit when I can to document the trip, so we can look back and talk about it to people and friends when he's older. Do you know how much longer it'll be before we land?"

"We should touch down in six hours," the man said. "Well, if you need anything let me or another crew member know because we're here to help."

"That's very nice. Okay, thanks, if anything comes to mind, I will."

Who's never been on a plane before? Michael thought. *Why did she say that? I think she's talking about me, but I've flown on a lot of planes. It feels like something familiar is happening here. Is this a dream?*

His senses became acute, the sounds around him became intense, and the vibrations of the plane's engines were now surging through his muscles and bones. The more he tried making sense out of it, the harder it was to realize what was happening, it all felt like a dream and real.

Where are we going? Where have I been? He raised his hand; it was small, then he moved his tiny fingers. *How old am I?* he thought. *My hand is so small! Looks like a baby's hand.* He watched the hand and fingers moving. *I've got to be dreaming!*

There was a man's voice again. "How is he? And how are you doing?" It was a different man that asked this time, and this voice Michael recognized for some unknown reason.

"Fine, we're okay here," the woman said.

"Are you excited about living in the United States?"

"I really am," she said.

I know those voices, then felt something underneath his back, then was lifted in front of the face of a woman, and could see her up close. *This lady sounds like she's got an accent,* he thought. The woman was talking to a man who had a different accent. *He sounds American, and she, German. Wait a minute I think she's my . . . Yes, it's her, my mother. How is this possible? How can I be here, seeing her here? How can I be flying in a plane and know what's happening if I'm only a baby? None of this makes any sense.*

Michael's head turned toward the man's speaking. "Can't say I like theses seats," the man said, and sat down. "Someday they'll design seats that are more comfortable."

"Better than not having seats," the woman said. "At

least we're not sitting on the floor."

I agree with her, better than not having seats, but how do I know that?

The man moved around getting comfortable in the seat. "Well, after landing in New York we'll have one night at a hotel, and won't have to worry about airplane seats for a while. Then in no time be on a train home, and then it's just a short drive back to the farm."

New York? Train home? Farm? I don't recall this, Michael thought.

"I'm looking forward to meeting your family," the woman said.

"And I know they're excited to meet and see you, too," the man said.

"I've told them all about you, so they're looking forward to seeing you, and of course, little Michael."

What are their names, Michael thought. *If I'm little Michael, is he big Michael?*

"Look at him smile," the man said. "He's feeling good, and looks happy. I wonder what he's thinking."

I'm thinking and wondering why I'm here. What's going on? This is crazy because I'm not a baby, but here I am in a baby's body.

"We'll have to go back to Austria someday in the near future," the woman said, "and visit my family after he grows up. Or perhaps we can invite the family here? Everyone will be surprised at how he's grown, and changed after they see him after a time."

"Maybe we can go back in a year or two," the man said, "but won't be staying long. Just a visit I think. Are you worried about living in the States? You don't have to be because you'll have my family, and relatives to help you with anything you need."

"Just a little worried; everything is going to be so different," the woman said. "But I'll be fine." She caressed the babies head, then gave him a bottle.

"Look at him go to town," he's a hungry guy," the man said.

"What's the place like?" the woman asked."Is it way in the country?"

"The family has two farms," he said, "and they're called the upper and the lower. The upper farm is for beef cattle, and the lower is the dairy. My uncle always raised herfords, and he keeps a huge bull, calls it Duke, not sure if it's still alive. There's another separate section of land called, The Forty, near the river used as pasture, and where there's a small grass runway with three hangers to park three planes. The man who owns one of the planes shows up every so often, and he'll be gone a few days or a month at a time. He also helps the farmers with flyovers to check their land and cattle. He took me up in his plane when I was a kid, that was my first time to fly in a plane, and I used to go fishing in the river near there."

"It all sounds peaceful living out in the countryside," the woman said.

"You have so many memories growing up there. What's the nearest town like?"

"The nearest town is actually more like a village. It's called Hungry Point, and basically a post office, small grocery store, and a bar where locals hang out."

"I can't wait to see it," the woman said. "I'm closing my eyes and resting now before we land. Can you wake me up when we get close and ready to land? I'd like to see it from the air."

I will," the man said. "I'll hold the baby for a while, you rest, you'll need later."

The man took the baby from the woman, cradled, and rocked him, then Michael looked at the man's face, and thought, *Things will different this time*.

THE NEXT DAY

The alarm clock buzzer echoed like a siren warning impending doom, and this continued for a while, it stopped, then the same process in a similar sequence started again. Michael stirred, opened his eyes with a wide long lasting yawn inhaling oxygen. Breathing in and out like a vacuum cleaner removing and filling his lungs with fresh air he didn't get up, and lay in bed for a time just taking more deep breaths.

Finally he moved leisurely, fumbled around trying to find the blaring clock without really looking, his hand just blindly explored while thinking, *Was I really flying on a plane or was that a dream? Sometimes it seems so real!*

Michael looked around the room not sure where he

actually had woken up. Eyes glazed he said, "It sure seemed real. Wow! What a crazy dream."

Checking the room again he noticed how the light streamed in and around the room from the gaps in the middle and sides of the closed curtains. *Light is what I remember from my dream*, he thought, then knocked over the clock and watched it fall to the floor howling, a noisy clanging alarm without missing a beat.

Michael grunted, moaned, sat up, grabbed the clock, switched it off and fell back on the bed. *Sue?* he thought, and noticed she was not there in the bed, but heard music coming from the kitchen, and her voice singing along to the song that was playing, then she stopped.

A few minutes later she appeared in the bedroom doorway. "Are you sleeping in today," she asked. "You're sleeping late today, and that's unusual for you. Don't remember the last time you did that."

Michael pulled his legs around and dropped his feet on the floor. "How long have you been up?" he asked, while rubbing his face and clearing the morning sleep from his eyes. "What time is it?" Yawning again, he stretched his arms out, turned, and cracked his neck left, then right. "I smell food cooking, and coffee brewing. It's making me hungry."

"What is it? Something wrong?" Sue asked wondering why he didn't know the time. "You've got a clock right there in your hands. Haven't you looked at it? Didn't you hear it? I heard it ringing."

"No, guess I haven't looked at it." he said, then blinked a couple of times and glanced down at the clock. "Time to get up, that's what time it is, I guess."

"I've already been up for a couple of hours," she said. "Just didn't want to wake you because you looked so cute curled up sleeping just like a baby."

Her baby remark triggered something from the dream he'd had. Michael grabbed a tissue, blew his nose, and sat quietly on the bed as images of a baby from the dream flashed in his head. *Funny she said, Sleeping like a baby.* he thought. Images of being on a trip to somewhere appeared, and he remembered voices, thinking that it may have been his mother and father talking on an airplane, but wasn't sure.

Although he remembered there was a conversation that he'd listened to during the dream nothing was lucid, only a few minor bits and pieces were retained. There was one part or episode where he remembered being lifted, then raised up and seeing a woman's face. This was vivid and real, but even that soon faded, was erased from memory, and only a washed out outline of a face remained.

"You okay," Sue said. "Looks like you're deep in thought. What are you thinking about? Michael? Hey, snap out of it! Are you sick?"

He shook his head, took a deep breath, and stared at Sue. "I'm fine, just remembering the dream I had last night. It's funny that you said I looked like a baby sleeping because I remember in my dream I was a baby, at least I think it was me. Well, physically a baby, but mentally grown up aware of my surroundings and wondering what was happening. I was watching people around me and felt myself there. I could hear the people, and we were on a plane flying somewhere. I couldn't talk, only think of what I wanted to say, and felt like I was in different places at the same time, changing from body to body at different ages of my life."

"That's a lot," she said. "You remember more of your dreams than I do. I usually forget everything I dream about. Of course there are times or things I occasionally recall, and wonder if there must be some meaning connected to it, but nothing seems to happen, and the dreams always end up a little blank."

"I've read about meaning in dreams, and only remember some parts of mine too. Not all of it comes back, just bits and pieces that don't make any sense. It's like a big puzzle, and never enough to make a connection or complete a comprehensible story."

"Tell me more about what you do remember," Sue said.

"First, I woke up on an old noisy plane flying over water I think, then discovered I was a baby after seeing my tiny hands, and heard people talking about me in the dream."

"You were a baby flying a plane?"

"No, not flying the plane, flying on a plane. A baby can't fly a plane. I was on it with people who I think were my parents."

"Your dream was about your parents?"

"First, I saw and heard a woman. I think she was my mother, but have no image of it, and can remember seeing a man. Or a man who I thought was my dad, maybe it was just from hearing his voice. Maybe I saw his face right before I woke up. The people were talking about something, but it's vague, and can't remember what was said. Think it was them, now I'm not sure. I don't know. Who else could they have been?"

"But you told me that you have no memory of your parents. How could they be in your dream if you have no idea of what they look or sound like? Usually the people in our dreams are from some encounter or experience I think. You don't remember any of what they said?"

"Bits are coming back, something about family, a conversation about people and a farm. I remember something about farms and cattle." Michael said.

"Meeting relatives, too, and I recall them talking about a river, but I can't remember the rest. I don't know what farm, though. I've never lived on a farm as far as I know. Maybe Poppi did, but I don't remember him ever mentioning it, at least nothing comes to mind."

"I think you're remembering quite a bit from your dream," Sue said.

"More than me, anyway. I hardly remember much at

all from my dreams."

"It's funny about the farm because no one's ever talked about a farm as far as I know," Michael said. "That part of the dream is hazy."

"You should ask Moses," Sue said. "He talked and spent a lot of time with your grandfather. Could have mentioned something about a farm to him."

"Moses started working for him later, after he built the cabin, and he already was doing mason work at that time. There doesn't seem to be any connection with a farm, don't remember cows, and he hired Moses because there was too much work to do. Couldn't keep up, at least that's what I heard him say when I was a kid."

"I guess you would know."

"So, what are you doing today?" Michael said, changing the topic.

"Just planning to finish up with unpacking, putting stuff away, and going for a run with Lori, the girl that works at the fitness center. She said I can get a discount if I join. Maybe you can get a one too if you come along."

"Never been a member a gym. I get enough exercise throwing stone and bricks around, and doing other construction work. But you should join, be careful though, don't want the little one tossed around."
"I'm sure the baby will be fine," Sue said. "I'm not planning to do anything too strenuous, just maintain where I am."

"And where you are," Michael siad, "is what I like."

"What about you?" Sue asked. "So, what are your plans for today?"

"I'm meeting Moses at a job site near here in fact, so we can have dinner tonight after if you like."

"Here at the apartment, or do you want to go out?" Sue asked.

"Let's just whip up something here," Michael said. "I can pick up anything we need. I'll even help make it."

"Don't worry about it," Sue said, "I'll get what we need. Let me surprise you. What time will you be back?"

"Could be back around six, but if I think I'll be late, I'll give you a call."

"Okay," she said, "It's settled."

"I'm jumping in the shower, then heading out to the job. Will you be here when I get out?"

"Yeah, I'll be here," Sue said. "Why wouldn't I?"

"I just remembered that time you disappeared, and I went crazy looking for you."

"Don't worry," Sue said. "I'll be here." They embraced, he went into the bathroom to shower. Sue watched as he closed the door and thought, *Something is going on here.*

BONE BREAKER

The football game was scheduled to start at 6:00 pm, and Michael was late, so he had to leave his car at the end of the parking lot far away from the stadium. He didn't want to miss anything, and wanted to see the game from the opening, so he decided to take what looked like a shortcut to ensure he could make the kick-off.

After checking the time he thought, *I'll never make the kick-off,* then saw a concrete wall that looked like a short cut. *I should be able to jump that wall. It looks easy to get over. Maybe I can still make the opening of the game if I hurry, and jumping that wall might save time. I think I can do it.*

He picked up the pace running at full bore, then braced

his hands on the wall, pushed up, and swung his legs over the wall. His face held a surprised frozen look, then shock took over and his face turned pale. Now he really felt stupid because of what he had just done.

"No, no, no!" was all he had time to yell after seeing that there was a twelve foot or so drop on the other side. The fall seemed timeless and lasted what seemed endless, so he planned a precise landing in his head. First, his feet contacting the ground falling forward rolling like a Ninja after hitting the ground, then jumping to his feet, and finally brushing himself off. As much as he tried to make it happen, reality set in, and he landed with all of his weight on his right leg.

Then heard some strange cracking breaking sounds, saw stars and blacked out for a time unknown. After re-gaining consciousness, he was flat on his back, and the first thought was, *Get up! Getup!* He rolled over onto his stomach, and from a prone postion with hands planted flat, pushed his chest off the ground up to his knees, then tried to stand. A lightning bolt of pain shot through his shattered leg, and he collapsed to the ground.

My leg is done for, he thought, *and there's no one around.* After a few minutes of being flat on the ground wondering what had really happened to his leg he glanced down at it, but from just a cursory observation nothing looked different or odd, as far as he could tell. Even though it looked fine he knew that wasn't the case and sat up, grabbed his pant leg, and rolled it back from his ankle. He stared and the bone protruding from the skin of his shin. *Oh, man, I'm so screwed!*

He'd never experienced an accident like this, and thought about his options, first he turned in his head, and took out his phone to call 911. While he did that a few people walked by and one person stopped.

"Are you all right buddy?" the man asked.

"Alright? I don't think so," Michael said. "Look at my leg. It's all messed up. I've got a bone sticking out of my skin."

"Holy crap!" the man said. "It looks pretty bad, and making me feel sick. I'll call 911. Just stay there on the ground and don't move."

"No need to phone," Michael said. "I just called, and they're already on the way."

"What can I do for you?" the man asked. "You want a drink of water?"

Then a few more people stopped to see what was going on. "I think it's better if you don't move," the man said.

By now a few security people had shown up, and were telling the people to continue walking by. Soon there were more security people, and more of a crow had gathered.

"What happened here?" one security person asked.

"I did something stupid, wanted to take a short cut, and thought I could jump over the wall. I didn't know it was such long drop on this side. I've dialed 911, and they're sending an ambulance."

"We've got medical people here at the stadium," a security guard said,

"I'll call them, just remain still, don't move."

"Guess, I'll leave," the first man who stopped said. "Looks like you've got plenty of help now. Good luck to you, pal."

As the man left a siren rang out, and they all turned toward the sound.

"They won't be able to drive up to here, so they'll park and bring a stretcher," a security guard said. "Look, here comes the calvary! They'll fix you up." Two paramedics with a stretcher, and bags of emergency quipment trotted over. "What happened here?"

"It's my leg," Michael said. "I did something really stupid. I jumped over that wall there, and didn't know the drop was so far down on the other side. I landed on my right leg with all of my weight, heard a snap, and it doesn't feel too good now. In fact I think I'm beyond feeling pain, and into a world of a painless non-feeling time."

"Okay, let's have a look," one paramedic said. "Yeah, that's a pretty long fall, and you really did a number on your leg. We'll take care of it."

***

Michael woke up at home, he looked around the room thinking, *This isn't a hospital?Didn't I jump over a wall and break my leg?* Then he looked at his leg. *It looks fine. Was that all a dream? Who was the guy with the broken leg? Was it me? Someone else? I don't remember seeing a face or did I? This is weird.*

He closed his eyes a moment, and tried to imagine how things had played out up to now, reliving the whole thing from what he remembered, but the gaps were wide and a lot of parts disconected. He concetrated deeply focusing on the jump over the wall hoping that it might trigger some memory of the dream.

"How about some breakfast?" Sue asked as she stood in the doorway of the room.

"Michael turned, jolted back a moment, and looked around again.

"I'm not at the apartment? When did we come back to the cabin?"

"What," Sue said. "We met after you finished working with Moses at the job site. You said you changed your mind and wanted to go to eat. We had a few drinks last night, but nothing to the degree that would make you forget how or when we got here. You remember that, right?"

Michael had a blank look for a moment, then said, "Oh yeah, it's coming back," he said, but still seemed confused at how he'd gotten to the cabin in Hungry Point from being at a football game and breaking a leg.

Sue walked over to the bed and sat near the edge. "Are you sure you're okay? You've got the same look you had that time in the car, when we were followed by the guys after eating at Reds. I have to say the way you're acting is getting more and more weird."

"Yeah," he said. "I'm fine."

"How about some coffee?" Sue asked.

"Nothing I'd like more, thanks," he said, and flopped back down on the bed.

"You're not getting up?"

"I'll get up soon," he said, "just need some time to get the morning cobwebs out. I'll go to the kitchen, you don't have to bring it in here, just let me have a minute to sort out my thoughts."

After a bit Michael got up, first, he tested his leg to make sure it was stable because he still had strong thoughts about it being broken. He put weight on it, jumped slightly, and found it stable. *Seems fine, that dream was so real. Who was the guy with the broken leg in my dream if it wasn't me? Why do I think that guy in my dream was me? Why does it seem like it really happened when it was only a dream?*

Walking into the kitchen the smell of brewing coffee, fried eggs, and toast floated through the air. Standing in the entryway he examined the kitchen seeing everything in its place just like it was supposed to be.

"Sit down, and here you go," she said, then put the coffee in front of him.

"This should wake you up, and there's more if you like."

"Where did you find this," he said looking the camouflage green cup with a picture of a T-Rex on the side. "I bought this when we went to Universal Studios years ago."

"Years ago?" Sue said. "It hasn't been that long."

"When was it?" Michael asked.
"Last summer, you're putting me on. You really don't remember?"

"Not clearly, not exactly, that was only last summer, seems longer. I do remember some of trip there, and I bought a cap."

"What did I say to you that day when you bought it?" Sue asked.

"What did you say?" Michael asked.

"Yeah, what did I say?" Sue said. "You don't remember, do you?"

"Yes, I do," he paused. "You said," Michael thought deeply, quietly concentrating, trying to focus, and force out the memory of that day.

"Wasn't it something about chocolate?"

"Well, not exactly about chocolate, but something to do with chocolate I guess in one way or another."
"Now I remember," Michael said. "You said, I think, that there should be a Dinosaur Day like Valentine's Day because you remembered that I liked dinosaurs"

"That's right," she said. "Very good, very good. Remember anything else?"

"Let me think," he said. "Something about it being my lucky day, I think."

"That's right," she said. "Do you remember why?"

"I found something that day," he said. "What did you find?"

"I remember now, a strange but an interesting looking stone, really smooth with gold lines that went around it. Looked like gold anyway. I don't remember what I did with that stone. I put it somewhere.

"You kept it, then brought it here?" Sue asked. "I don't know where you put it. You don't remember?"

"Probably in one of the boxes of junk that I keep in the storeroom."

"There were some symbols on it," Sue said. "Shapes I'd never seen before, and you said the same thing, that the shapes were so unusual, but familiar because you had seen them before."

"Yeah, I did see them somewhere. Say, you want to go for a walk later," Michael said. "Go see the river just like old times."

"Okay, let's eat first, then take a walk through the woods down to the river."

SEARCH FOR THE BEGINNING

Looking up above to an endless blue sky in total view, and completely visible, while panning across the river of apple blossoms, covering and wrapping rolling hills of an endless valley below that echoed with the sounds of nature.

Soaking in all of the surrounding beauty Sue wondered how long watching these images of seasons changing would last, then after she blinked it was dark.

The darkness with intermitent flashes of light and rumbling continuned, softened, then vanished. And after what seemed only a moment, she opened her eyes, smiled, and was held up for all to see. *Am I in a hospital?* But soon this hospital image faded, she had awaken and was carried to another place, set down, and left looking up from under what she thought was a table.

After a little longer she was peering at a face. And a smiling man's face looking back at her with eyes of surprise. "Where did you come from?" Of course she couldn't answer his qusetions because being a baby, and knowing she had probably just been born a time earlier, could only manage intermediary crying.

As she looked around could make out it was a dimly lit place. Walls were covered with bottles stacked on shelves in front of a reflective surface, so she could see the back of them. In view high on the wall near the ceiling, trophys were lined up, and all surrounded by a recognizable odor, perhaps a combination of smoke and beer, as lights fixed all around glowed in abient light.

How do I know the names and what these things are called?

She looked again at trophys lined up on shelves high on the walls surrounding the room. There seemed to be clutter all around, on the tables, some dishes, leftover food, and some cards spread under a deck with poker chips. Two pool tables set up with balls racked for the next players, music playing a song that she remembered, but the name forgotten.

Jeremiah Kick looked around the bar trying to catch sight of anyone who might be there, but the bar was empty. "What should I do with you?" He picked up the basket, placed it on top of table, and stepped back. "I don't know anything about babies. Who can I call for help?" Then he thought, *Maria, she might know what to do.*

Maria worked at the bar for Kick. She was in her mid-thirties, slim, left her curly brown hair in a natural way, was single, and always dressed smartly. Kick spent a lot of time with her working in the bar, camping and fishing. He dialed her number, and thought, *I hope she can help.*

The phone rang, no answer, but just as Kick was about to hang up he heard a voice.

"Hello."

"Maria, sorry for calling you so late, I'm glad your still be up. You have a minute? I've got a problem, and need your help."

"I'm fine, it's okay calling. What's wrong?" she asked. "Are you okay? Did something happen after I left bar tonight? Sorry for leaving early."

"Well something did kind of happen, and I really don't know what to do." Kick said. "Nothing about working at the bar, but I need some advice, and thought you could help."

"I'll try to help if I can," she said. "What do you need?"

"Well after you left I started cleaning up a little, you know to make it easier tomorrow, and you're not going to believe what I found."

"If it's money it's mine," she said, and laughed. "So,

how much did you find?"

"I wish it was money," he said. "I was cleaning up the glasses, bottles, and cans from the tables when I heard a noise."

"What kind of noise?"

"At first I thought it was a puppy, sounded like that anyway, then I looked under a table."

"And what did you find under the table?"

"I found a baby," he said. "A tiny little baby."

"A baby!" she said, "Really? A little baby?" and thought he was joking, but then realized he would never joke about something like this.

"Yeah, a little baby," Kick said. "I've got her here right in front of me, and haven't got any stuff to take care of a baby. I thought, you being a woman might know, and could tell me what to do."

"I haven't had the experience of raising kids, but have babysat quite a bit. You want me to go back to the bar? I can be there in about thirty minutes."

"Yeah, that would be good I think," he said. "Can you come right now, and bring some things we might need?"

"I'll make some calls, get some basic baby things, be there soon."

"Thanks," Kick said, hung up, and looked at the baby

who now was asleep.

"I'm tired too kid. I'm tired too." Kick's bar was the only place to get a late night drink, and something to eat in Hungry Point. He had a room above the bar that he used when he didn't feel like going to the farm. He had taken over the place from his father after he died, and maintained the family farm where he grew corn, soybeans, and a few other crops.

I guess I'll keep her here tonight and call the police tomorrow.

Kick continued cleaning up while keeping an eye on the little visitor, and was sweeping when Maria showed up. "Hey, thanks for helping out."

"That's what friends do for each other," she said. "Where's the bundle?"
"Right there on the table, a baby, sleeping like a baby."

"Let's have a look at the little one," Maria said, and put down the bag of supplies she'd brought, then stood over the basket that held the baby. "So cute, so cute."

"I agree, cute, but what should we do now? This has never happened to me. I have no idea about what to do."

"Can't do anything tonight," Maria said, "it's too late. Just keep her here until tomorrow, then call the police I guess. They'll tell us what to do after that. They'll probably take her to children's services."

"Should we go upstairs?" Kick said. "More

comfortable up there for us. So, what things did you bring for the baby?"

"All that stuff in the bag over there," Maria said. "Some diapers, a couple of bottles, some baby food because I wasn't sure how old she was, and some other things that might be useful. I'll take her, and you grab the bag."

"Okay, got it, let's go," he said. "I wonder what will happen to her."

"Well," she said, "they'll probably try to find her parents. I'm sure it's a crime to abandon and leave a baby alone. If they can't find her parents or next of kin I'd guess she'll be put up for adoption."

"How does that work," he asked. "Can anyone adopt her if it comes down to that?"

"I don't know myself, I've never adopted a baby or children, but don't worry, it'll all be fine."

"Do you believe destiny?" Kick asked.

"You think the baby being left at your place for some reason? A higher force left the baby at your bar?"

"Well, yeah, I mean, how often does something like that happen, especially in Hungry Point. Never as far as I know."

"I see what you're getting at, but things happen for many reasons, and sometimes we never know why.

No one has all of the answers, but we always have questions it seems."

"Here, let me get the door," he said. "Is she still asleep?"

"Yes, still sleeping," Maria said. "It's good, but she'll wake up and want something to eat in time, so if you're tired, and want to get some rest, I'll watch her."

"I don't think I can sleep," Kick said.

"Suit yourself," she said. "Then I'll make a sandwich and you keep an eye on her. Want one?"

"Sure, sounds good."

***

So, as it turned out Kick adopted the baby, named her Sue, and she grew up helping Kick at the farm and bar. As far as she knew up to now, she was Kick's daughter. The farm was near Hungry Point and the river. Kick had grown up there helping his dad J. Kick on the farm. He learned how to drive tractors, pick-up trucks, and finally saved up for a motorcycle, and planned to pass it all on to Sue.

While going to school Sue became friends with Michael, growing up together, spending time on the river, camping, hiking, fishing, and talking about dreams. Then one day when Sue was ten years old driving back from a fishing trip, he told her the story of how he found her under a table at the bar.

The truck rolled down the country road. This was the same truck they always used on camping and fishing trips. It was rusty, had peeling paint, and was noisy as it rumbled down the road, but the engine never failed. They were both unusally quiet on the way back this time, and Kick wondered why Sue seemed sullen. There wa no music playing, but Sue was tapping her hands to the beat of a song.

"A quiet day today, Sue. What are are you thinking about?"

She paused, looked at Kick, then turned back to look out the window. "Kick, I've always felt like there's something you've want to tell me, but are waiting for the right time."

"What makes you think that?"

"Been building up a while now, and just think there is something I should know. Well, things like, why I don't have a mother? Not even a picture of her anywhere, and no one I talk to knows anything about her. It doesn't take a genius to figure out something is funny."

"I guess you're old enough to know the story, so I'll do my best, just come right out and tell you what happened as I know it. First, it's correct that I'm not your real father, and you have a mother somewhere. I have never seen or met her, and no one knows where she is or if she's even alive. You have a father, but don't know where he is either."

Sue looked out the window of the truck again watching fence posts glide by, then turned toward Kick. "Who am I then? What's my real name? Do I have any brothers or sisters? Will I ever know?"

Kick paused a moment. "You're Sue Kick, my daughter, and I think you know will always be my daughter."

"How did I become Sue Kick?"

"I found you at the bar under a table after closing one night. I was cleaning, and heard some whimpering sounds, then found you in a basket under a table. At first after hearing some wimpering I thought you were a puppy. After taking a closer look, found you i a basket."

"You didn't find anyone or hear anything after? Was there a note or letter?"

"Nothing, just you. I called a friend to help, and she brought some things over. The next day I called the police, they took you and investigated, but discovered nothing about your background. Then you were put up for adoption, so I got in for the adoption because there had to be a reason for you being there. And here you are with me. I have daughter and her name is Sue."

Sue smiled and thought of the song with a similar name. "Is that why you like that song so much? Am I named after a song?"

"I like that song, but love the name."

"Do you still think there's a reason for that happening? For me being left at the bar?"

"Yes, I do. You have a purpose, and somehow I'm supposed to help you be successful or find out why it happened. I know it's sounds strange, but I really believe that. You have been the best thing that's ever happened to me."

Sue smiled, and draped her arm around Kick while leaning on his shoulder. "You're the best thing that's happened to me, Kick."

He grinned. "We'll figure all of this as it comes, and just take it day by day. I want to help you become whatever it is you dream to be. I think there's a special plan for you."

"You really think so?"

"Of course, and you spend a lot of time with Michael. Maybe you guys will do something great in the future."

ADOPTION   REVISITED

Sue had graduated from high school and was taking it easy for the summer while thinking about what the future held for her. She'd been waking up late almost every summer morning up to now, and taking advantage of the time off, but for some reason on this particular morning she was up early.

Birds were chirping as she lay still on her bed looking at the ceiling, stretching and yawning to get more oxygen to jump start her muscles, body, and mind.

She visually scanned all of the objects around the room while remembering where she'd gotten them. After a bit her focus zoomed toward the window frame, then through the glass and outside, where the biggest tree in the yard sat directly in view. The branches rocked to some mysterious rhythm in the early morning breeze, the leaves fluttered, a few fell and glided slowly finally resting on ground.

She tossed off the blanket, stood, dropped her arms down to the sides of her legs and bent down touching her toes. After counting to ten she stood, and ended the move with her arms above her head pointing straight to the ceiling. With the next move, and hands to her sides again, she raised her shoulders up to her ears a couple of times, then pulled her arms behind her back, palms touching, then raised her arms to the ceiling again. After a time of silence she made herself comfortable on the yoga mat in the middle of the room, and for about thirty minutes continued the usual stretching routine, then went into the kitchen and brewed some coffee.

She wasn't sure what was coming next in her life, so in the meantime the plan was to stay on with her stepfather, Kick, help him run the bar until she figured things out, and then hopefully decide on what to do.

There were other options and varies opportunities to do almost anything she wanted, the world was waiting for her to grab and take her piece of the pie. As these thoughts crossed her mind, other than being with Michael, she really wasn't sure what she would do with her future life.

On this early lazy morning a bevy of ideas flowed through her head, things like the river she had lived next to, and how things can go down or up stream in life just like in the river. Then the dreamlike state she'd been immersed in was broken when she noticed a car driving down the road in front of the house.

It stopped at the end of the driveway next to the mailbox. She watched the mailman drop a stack of letters and papers into it and drive away. For a moment her eyes were fixed on the car driving away, then darted to the mailbox. *Guess I can see what's there.*

After a moment she made her way to refrigerator, opened it to see what there was to eat, and grabbed two eggs. She poured herself a fresh cup of coffee, then after taking a sip put two eggs in a pan and fried them sunny side up.

The toast popped up, she flipped the eggs, then a moment later was sitting at the table eating. She always sat in the same place as far back as she could remember, and when she looked up there it was just like always, an upright horseshoe nailed and hanging above the door.

Will today be a good lucky horseshoe day?

She washed the dishes, drank one more cup of coffee, then made her way outside and down the driveway still wearing the blue-jean shorts and the t-shirt she'd slept in.

As she screened the mail, found the newspaper, a local shopper paper filled with ads with things for sale. There was some junk mail, and an official looking envelop with a law firm's address and her name on the front. *What's this?* she thought, looking it over, checking the address, and wondering why her name was on an envelope from a law firm.

She went back into the house still wondering why she'd received a letter like this, and put the other mail on the kitchen table, then torn off the flap on the envelope. Sue pulled out a letter with a few other documents, scanning them, then she checked more carefully to make sure that the letter was indeed addressed to her.

Ms. Kick,

Let me introduce myself, my name is R. Lee, and I work for a private investigation firm. We were hired by our client to search for you, and that's what we've done. Now, that said, I'm sure you're wondering why my firm was hired for that purpose, and the only thing I can say may surprise you. So, that said, I won't hold you in suspense any longer and be candid. One last thing, you may want to sit down when you read the next part of the letter.

Okay, my firm was contracted and retained by your parents, and they would like to meet you. This is where you read the last sentence again, after that take a couple of deep breaths, and yes, I said your parents. And also, this is not a joke, it's authentic, and I'm certain you'll have many questions to ask.

I've looked into your situation,

according to the request of the people who say they are your parents. Up to now you've believed that your parents were killed in a car accident, but I can assure you that is not what happened.

I'm not sure if or what information your step-father, Mr. Kick, has shared or told you about any of this, so here we go, let me tell you what I know. I'll explain in more detail to fill gaps that you may have questions about. I don't have all of the answers, but will try to shed as much light on your situation as possible.

According to the records we've uncovered, I've discovered that you were given up for adoption after birth by your mother. She being a young woman and a student at the time, felt she could not bring up a child alone. Of course the details of how and where you were left abandoned are a little cloudy. But your father not knowing anything about this had left, started a company which today has become quite successful.

After birth you were immediately given up as a ward of the state, and put into an adoption program. Again we're not sure how you ended up with Mr. Kick, but that said he is or was your legal guardian.

So, after your birth father finding this out recently has decided that he'd like to meet you, and try make up for lost time. As far as your mother goes we don't have any new information of what happened to her.

I'm sure after hearing this you have a lot of questions. My contact information is on the business card I've included with this letter. If you'd like to talk more about it we can arrange a meeting at your convenience. I've also included some copies of photos that were taken of you at birth, and other documents of proof of identification.

So, it's all up to you now to what happens next. You have my information, and if you wish to contact me, do so at your convenience.

Best Regards,
R. Lee

Sue put the letter on the table and just looked at it not knowing how to deal with such news. The shock of what she'd read made her numb.

Who should I call? Who should I tell? She picked up her phone and dialed Michael's number.

The phone rang a couple of times, then she heard Michael's voice. "Hi, morning, what's going on?"

"What are you up to?"

"Heading to a job to help fix a barn for a farmer. How about you?"

"Just got the mail and having something to eat. Can you talk?"

"What's on your mind?

"What time will you finish?"

"Probably late, but not sure, but Moses is looking at me now with a don't skip out, and have to help him the whole day look."

"Can we meet later?"

"Six or so would be good I guess. Want to meet up later?"

"Yes, I do, and have to show you something."

"What's that?"

"I can't tell you, have to show you because it's too hard to explain."

"Wow, you sound a little mysterious," he said. "What's this all about?"

"It knocked me back, and for a whirl, and do the same to you I think."

"Really, this must be some wild news."
"I don't know if it's under the category of fantastic, but it's pretty wild."

"Now, I'll be thinking about it the rest of the day until you tell me."

"Where do you want to meet?"

"At the bar I guess, we can have a pizza."
Have you shared this news with anyone else?"

"No, you'll be the first to hear about it."

"Okay, leaving for the work site now, so let's talk later." Michael said.

"See you later."

"Bye."

"You done talking now?" Moses asked

"Yeah, hey, she has some big news, but wouldn't say what it was."

"Big news!" Moses said. "What's going on?"

"She mentioned she got something in the mail that surprised her? We're meeting later at the bar. Want to join us for pizza?"

"Pizza," Moses said. "Don't have to ask me twice as long as it's okay with Sue. Let's head to the job site, get that done, and go for pizza."

WALL PAPER

Wonders and mysteries are widespread, run throughout an unknown unlimited universe, on other planets, and here on earth. We read and study about this from a young age.

Our surroundings and schools teach us about the human race, but we really haven't discovered the key to any of it, and the secrets we seek remain hidden and unknown. Clues are all over the place, so it's like putting together a great big puzzle.

Once a piece is found we try to figure out how it fits into the big picture. That's the difficult part because there's no blueprint for putting together the puzzle.

The planet earth has been explored by many, the mysteries appear, amaze us, and as time counts on new discoveries trickle like drops of water from a leaky faucet. We're left thinking over these new discoveries that stare us right in the face. We wonder why wasn't it found earlier?

Artifacts, bobbles and carvings are studied carefully with the notion that perhaps someday, or somehow, they can be traced or should lead back to a time of our ancestors and the origin of where we started. One day we will finally know the answer to these questions of where we come from, what our purpose in this endless universe of stars is, and what the future is ahead.

When it comes to human origin and a purpose there are different theories out there, but know one really can say unequivocally where humans come from, and we have no clue of the purpose we strive to accomplish. Basically at the root there are various camps, ideas, and opinions of the religious who vary in degree from zealot to agnostic.

Creationists believe humans are created by God, the evolutionists are of the opinion that humans come from apes and evolved into people, and those who believe aliens somehow mixed with humans on earth as an experiment just to see what would happen.

There are some who think aliens and apes bred and became a sort of hybrid alien human creature, and this might seem plausible if you consider that humans have a highly evolved brain that other species do not. All we know is that after the discovery of fire there was no turning back, and fire has created life that continuously evolves.

From research we've uncovered and discovered our forbearers could do unbelievable and amazing feats, and this includes examples of some of the most complex structures and construction sites that are prevalent tourist spots today.

Along with all of these examples are stone carvings mapping the solar system before any type of telescope was available at the time, and it was done by ancient cultures without any modern equipment. Secrets are buried everywhere, and to find them all we need do is look beneath our feet and above.

With careful examination we find images embedded everywhere, in wood grain, marble, wall paper, and most other patterns that were at one time camouflaged can now easily be seen.

This information is available to all who are interested, the curious, all who have the ability to judge wisely, and the chosen ones who can alter the information to their liking. This may not be a learned skill, but an ability one is born with, and slowly refines to the point where mind travel to other hidden worlds takes place.

Sounds impossible and beyond human comprehension for most, but this is only one part of the equation. For example we learn from nature; take the configuration of the snowflake. From close examination we know that every snowflake is a different size and shape, and no two are alike. The amazing thing about the snowflake is that we can actually see it with the naked eye.

With the equipment available now even the miniscule and previously invisible can now be examined. If John

Bell's theorem rings true, as to say, 1+1=3, the reality of nature, metaphysics, quantum mechanics, and reality in a non-local. This says that no physical theory of local hidden variables can ever reproduce all predictions of quantum mechanics.

Everything is determined by decisions, the parameters, sequence, length of time, temperature, and weight. Even the person controlling the experiment sways the outcome of what can happen as the decisions are made, and in what order or sequence.

**

"Where did you buy that wall paper?" Michael asked. "Found it at the DYI store," Sue said. "It has everything," she said, "and they've got so much to choose from. When I saw this one I fell in love with the color and pattern."

"Well it's interesting looking that's for sure, and if I squint, it looks like a lot of small bookshelves lined up. What's the wallpaper called?" Michael asked. "And who's putting it up?"

"I don't know what it's called, maybe Bookshelves, since that's the pattern. See, looks like bookshelves. I just like it, and thought we could do it together," she said. "You build stuff with wood and stone, so I imagine hanging some wall paper should be a breeze. You can do it, right?"

"Never done any wall paper hanging work," Michael said. "but I'm sure we can figure out how to put it up, and hopefully make it look good. How hard can it be?"

"What do we need to do first," Sue asked.

"Well the walls are painted, and they look smooth, so it just an application job I think. We shouldn't have to prep the walls much. We just have to make sure there aren't any bubbles when we put it on the wall."

"What do we use to stick it on the wall with?"

"Wall paper paste, and I've got plumb guide to make a grid to keep it straight, but we need some brushes for the paste. Some dry cloths, a trimming razor, something to hold water. Can find most of that stuff or buy it. We've got to make sure the ends match, align it from the top down, trim the top and bottom, and clean away any excess adhesive. Come to think of it, this might be tougher than I thought, maybe we should hire it out to someone."

"So, you don't want to try?"

"That's not what I said. We can do it. I'm just joking."

"Well when can we start?" Sue asked.

"As soon as you're ready," Michael said.

"I'm ready now," she said.

Michael started looking for the things they needed to do the job, but seemed to take his time. "Okay," Michael said. "Shouldn't take me long to get the stuff together, and we'll get going on this right away."

They worked on putting up the wall paper on the walls in the apartment all afternoon and into the night. Finally at around 1:00 a.m. they were finished, and it looked nice. They admired their work, celebrated with a glass of wine, and managed to drink the whole bottle. They talked about how they could change the other rooms, but always came back to the wall paper.

"This pattern you chose is quite interesting," Michael said. "If I stare at one spot it almost looks like there's an image hidden deep inside the pattern. It almost seems as if I could go into the wall."

"Where do you see an image?" she asked.

"Look at the corner there," he said, "then just to the left, about right in the middle. You don't see anything?"

"Not really," she said. "Where should I look?"

"Right there," he said and pointed, the walked over to the spot. "Right here."

"Sorry, I can't see a thing," Sue said, "only the pattern."

"Maybe if you squint you'll be able to see it?"

"Nope," she said. "Nothing. Can't see a thing other than wallpaper."

"Well, after a few glasses of wine an image might come out."

"I've had as many glasses of wine as you, and can't see anything other than the pattern."

"Well, it's there," Michael said. "If you look really hard you can see it."

"I'm trying, but just can't see anything," Sue said. "You must be doing more than just squinting. Have got some kind of x-ray vision."

"Well," Michael said, and smiled. "Try thinking deeply, holding a thought as long s possible, controlling your body, muscles, like when you do your Yoga exercises. You've done it before. I know it."

"Yoga?" Sue said, "is a hit and miss proposition. It's uncontrollable. A person never knows when they might be enlighted."

"Takes practice that's all," Michael said. "I see all kinds of images in the pattern, they change and move as I focus. I can see deeply into the patterns, beyond the surface, peeling layers back, uncovering what most cannot see."

"You've never spoken like this before. Is this something new you started and practice?

"I've been learning, studying, wondering why things are the way they are, and I see something in the wall paper pattern, and in other patterns too. It happens when I'm making something out of random stones, blocks and bricks. "

"Is there a name for that?"

"Not sure if there is, but I know it exists. Lets look it up." Michael checked his phone. "Here we go, it's called pareidolia."

DRIVE TO CALIFORNIA

Michael woke up behind the wheel of his car, at least he thought it must be his car, why else would he be sitting it. Looking around the interior things he saw were familiar, a canteen, black windbreaker jacket, a camera, a book of poems, some maps. Even with knowing this he seemed to have lost some connection to how he had gotten, or why he was there.

Ahead was the wide open sky, with mountains in the distance, and tall trees all around. It was early morning, and the sun had just risen warming up the interior of the car, so he rolled the window down, leaned out and took a deep breath. To the right the western style water canteen that sat on the seat, so he grabbed, and swallowed enough of the precious clear liquid to quench his thirst.

Alone out in the middle of nowhere, not knowing the place where he currently seemed to have woken, or how he had gotten there continued to cross his mind. He opened the door and stepped out of the 1971 silver Dodge Challenger. *When did I get this car?* he thought, then images of someone handing money to a guy to pay for it, and who he thought must have been the owner appeared in his mind.

Then another image of driving away and ending up where he was now parked on the side of a road, and closing in on the foot of the Rocky Mountains. *Where am I?* he thought, and saw no other cars anywhere in sight as the morning air continued warming as the sun rose.

Michael felt hungry, but had no food to eat in the car, so he decided to drive down the highway looking for restaurant or cafe. He started the engine and felt power vibrate through the frame of the car, then as he drove could tell this was a fast car and memories behind the wheel appeared.

The mountains were getting closer and he felt as though they would always be out of reach, but he finally made it in after following thewinding steep roads. He contiuned driving without any destination in mind. *This scenery is spectacular*, he thought. *And I think I've seen it before.* These thoughts re-emerged as the rumbled up and down twisting narrow roads. *I'm in the middle of nowhere.*

In one sense he knew where to go and would find out the reason after arriving wherever that was. The high top mountains were a natural barrier to invaders, and without special effort could never cross over them. He wondered how pioneers back in the day were able to find a trail. Once he reached what seemed the top could see patches of snow pack not giving up the fight for winter, but since this was August it wouldn't last.

He pulled over to the side of the road to take in the vast expanse of the continental divide. This was something he read about and had seen pictues of in books, but that was nothing compared to being near the real thing. After some time there all alone just for that moment shook from the grandness, then got back into the car and set off down the mountain. Up the road a log building came in view with a sign out front, and when he closed in closer, could read what it said. The sign out in front attached on the log structure said, **Rocky Mountain Food**, and this log structure sat at the bottom of the mountain range under a blue sky with clouds floating by slowly, which made it look to be a winner of a location and day.

Guess I'll try that place, he thought. After parking he looked around again thinking he'd been in this place at some time before, but that's all, no other images or thoughts, just that he'd been there. While walking up the stone steps to the restaurant he seemed to be retracing or following his steps as they led up to a deck with some wooden tables and chairs, then he turned and glanced out toward the mountains where buffalo grazed in the distance.

He walked in to see breakfast was over and lunch was now being served. The place had a wooden counter, wooden tables and chairs, and Michael was drawn over to sit at a table in the corner for the some reason while feeling it wasn't the first time to be there.

Michael sat looking over the menu, then checking the restaurant, and it seemed familiar as well.

After a few minutes a waiter came over. "Coffee?"

"Sure, sounds great," Michael said. "Say, I'm not from here, and just wondering ,what the name of the nearest town?"

"I guess that would be Silverton," the waiter said.

"You know about how far it is?"

"About an hour to drive," he said, then asked if Michael was ready to order.

"Looks like it's a little late for breakfast, but can I still get a couple of fried eggs over easy and some toast?"

"Yeah, sure, no problem," the waiter said. "Anything else?"

"No, that's all."

"Okay, should be ready in ten minutes."

Customers came and went as Michael ate his lunch. Some wore caual clothes, a few were in cowboy hats, some had baseball caps, one or two in suits, and they seem to all be a group of hard workers. Michael thought of what these people did to make a living because he didn't see any factories as he drove there. He observed, listend to parts of the conversations he overheard which were about friends, relatives, and business.

One lady talked about her boyfriend being arrested a week ago for being drunk, another about a great deal on a car, and someone was commenting on the current politcal enviroment. On and on the people talked while he listened, and like other things he seemed to recall some of it, almost like listneing to a recoreding from the past. Then the waiter walked through asking if anyone wanted more coffee.

Michael signaled with a wave of his hand, and said, "Can you top mine off? Can I have my check?"

The waiter filled Michael's cup. "I'll get the check ready."

"Thanks," Michael said, then asked, "Are you from around here?"

"No, I'm just passing through. Needed some cash, so I took this job about six months ago. I was heading for L.A. How about you? Where are you from?"

"A small town you've never heard of called, Hungry Point."

"You're right, never heard of it. Where's that?"

"It's in Wisconsin."

"Wisconsin? Where's that? Just joking, you're a ways from home," the waiter said. "Here's your check, you can pay me when you're ready."

Michael left the restaurant and was back on the road heading to Silverton wondering why he was in this place, and why he had this car.

He tried to put together the pieces of a lost memory puzzle because there had to be a reason. Heading down the road he drove passed a guy walking who had his hand out, and thumb up hiking a ride.

Should I pick him up? Maybe he's a local who can tell me about the area.

Michael stopped and watched the guy walk up to car, then opened the door inviting him in the car. "Hi, there," Michael said. "Where are you heading?"

"Hi, thanks for stopping," the guy said. "I'm going to Los Angeles. How about you?"

"A lot of people are going to L.A. I'm going to the next town, Silverton."

"Okay if I ride along till Silverton?"

"Sure, okay, hop in."

"This is a nice car you've got," the man said. "Bet it's fast too."

"Yeah, a little, but all of the roads around here are narrow and twisting, so I can't really open it up No problem climbing the mountain."

The guy wore a cowboy hat, a denim coat, jeans, and

carried an army duffel bag with an aroma of patchouli oil following him.

"I see your plates are from Wisconsin," the man said. "What town are you from?"

"A small country place called Hungry Point."

"That's a funny name for a town. How'd it get that name?"

"I don't know," Michael said. "That's good question."

"What do you do in Hungry Point?"

"I'm a mason, work with stone, brick, and do construction work. How about you? What's in L.A.?"

"I want to get into acting, directing, that sort of thing." the hiker said.

"Well, that's the place to go," Michael said. "Lot's of movies made there. Good luck with it. You have any experience doing any of that?"

"I've always liked movies, especially whenever I've felt sick or down. I'd go to the movies, then always felt better, it seemed to be a good way to forget everything and just get lost."

"Look, there's the sign for Silverton," the hiker said. "Ten miles ahead."

As they entered the town none of the buildings in Silverton looked old, except for their design. It was like driving back through another dimension from the past.

Wooden buildings lined up in a row on both sides of Main Street with parking meters in the center for cars to park diagonally. One store had a big sign that said, Appliances, another Vogue Movie theater.

There was a General Store, and Michael had the same continuing feeling of being in this town at some time in the past.

"Where should I drop you off?"

"I guess anywhere will do. I'll walk around town a little, maybe stay the night. I'm sure there's a hotel of some kind or Bed & Breakfast around here."

"I'll pull into that service station up ahead, get some gas, and check over the car. That work for you?"

"That's fine for me. It was a short ride, but thanks. Good luck to you, have a good day."

Michael stopped the car. "Good luck to you, hope the movie thing works out for you. What's your name? Or what's your movie name going to be?"

"I'm Luke Paris. Everyone just calls me Paris."

After hearing that name Michael was overwhelmed and flooded with images, thoughts, and ideas. Paris got out of the car, then turned rested his arms on the window, and crouched down gazing at Michael.

"Hey pal you okay?"
Michael leaned forward, clasped his hands over his face massaging it. "Yeah, I'm fine, just had a bit of a dizzy spell for a moment."

"You need some help?"

"No, I'm fine," Michael said. "Just need a moment to compose myself."

"Are you sure you're going to be okay? You look a little pale. Have a swig of water."

Michael drank a little water, then felt better as the images stopped, but remembered floating through a covered space after a man who looked a like the hiker he'd picked up.

"Well, good luck to you, and I hope you are alright. You should park here for a while. I wouldn't head out until you are sure it's safe to drive. When was the last time you ate?"

"I ate right before I picked you up, just had some eggs, toast and coffee. I'm okay now." Michael got out, walked to the pump, and filled the tank. "Maybe we'll run into each other again. Good luck with the movie thing."

"Good luck to you," Paris said. "You can make your life whatever you want it to be," then as Michael watched, Paris walked across, down the street, and disappeared around the corner.

A VISIT TO THE LAB

Sue woke, looked over at Michael a moment, studied how he slept, then touched his shoulder thinking he'd wake up, but he didn't.

She continued to watch him stretch, moan, rolled over, and smile, then he looked out at the room through his heavy partially opened eyelids.

He looked around like he was lost or had woken up in an unknown place, everything looked different and unfamiliar.

"Hey, are you getting up?"

"Hi," Michael said, sounding groggy like a guy recovering from a hangover. "I think so, pretty soon."

Then he rolled over seemly going back to sleep.

"Morning," Sue said, again. "Are you getting up? You usually don't sleep so late. What's going on for you today? You feel hungry, like having breakfast, or early lunch?"

"Food sounds good, and if you're cooking," Michael said, "don't have to twist my arm. I know it'll be good."

"What do you feel like eating?"

"Anything you make is fine with me," he said.

"Eggs, toast, a cup of coffee?"

"Sounds perfect, you're reading my mind."

"Reading your mind? That's easy because you eat the same thing every morning," Sue said, and she was about to get out of bed when Michael reached out grabbing, catching, and pulling her back into the bed. Sue trying to escape Michael's grip said, "Come on, stop, it's late. We should get up."

"And you're beautiful," he said, then wrapped his arms around her in a bear hug. "Don't run off so soon, breakfast can wait."

She manipulated her body around to be more comfortable, and turned around until they were face to face. They kissed, rubbed noses, caressed each other, and in many ways until both of their spirits mingled, and tingled with exuberance. "Going to finish what you started," Sue asked.

Michael looked at Sue, kissed her, then said, "Nothing I like more than finish what I start."

With that they disappeared under the covers, and imagined a flock of bird's musical warbling singing out, the sound spinning up in the air as they dove to another place to a home sweet home of love. After a time later they lay there in bed looking up at the ceiling, silent, then he rolled over kissing and rubbing her cheek to cheek, landing on her as they rolled to the other side of the bed.

Michael laughed, then looked at Sue. "What are you doing today?
You just staying at home?"

"I made plans to meet up with my dad. I think I told you he's taking me on a tour of his company. Want to come along? I'm sure he'd be more than happy to show you around, and will probably ask again if you'd like to work for him. It could be an exciting place to work."

"Yeah, like to, but can't, and it's not that I don't want to, but I'm supposed to meet Moses in town this morning, then head to a job." He looked at the clock. "It's getting late. I'm sure Moses is already on the way there, and on the job site already. You can tell me all about the tour of your dad's company tonight. I'd better get going or Moses will be mad has hell."

"It's your business," Sue said.

"I know, but he's older than me, and does most of the work. Want to meet in town later and have dinner?"

"Okay, sounds good. I'll call you when I'm on my way back to town after I get back from the company," Sue said. "I'll have breakfast ready in bit. You can take your time." Sue stopped at the door, turned and said, "You have to actually get out of bed because I'm not bringing breakfast up here. Let's get moving!"

"Okay, okay," Michael said. "I'm going, I'm getting up. See you downstairs."

As the aroma of breakfast lingered the clanking of dishes and pans being washed was done, they walked out together and stood on the deck. Sue still in her pajamas as Michael grabbed her and held her close. "This is going to be a great day" Michael said. "I can feel it."

They stood arm in arm for what seemed an endless time, as if there was no time, without saying a word. The world didn't exist for them at this time, and they held each other in silence sharing thoughts.

"I'd better get going, Moses is waiting for me. He's always on time, and gets riled up when I'm late." After one more hug and kiss Michael got into his truck. Sue waved as he drove away, and turned to go into the cabin as a bell ringing sound echoed overhead.

After looking all around to find the sound's orgin, she saw nothing that could have made the sound, then a minute later she felt dizzy. Overwhelmed with images flashing through her mind while slowly step by step making her way back into the cabin.

She staggard to the sofa and collapsed.

***

Some time later she woke refreshed with only a slight memory of what had happened. *Did I have a dream? Must have, just can't remember it.* Sue got ready, and left to meet her dad at his company.

Sue liked driving Michael's mustang, and it had a sentimental connection being it was the first car he'd bought, so they spent a lot of time driving to different places in it. Sue read the directions to the company she had been given by her father, and followed the signs matching them to the map he'd sent. The drive to the company location looked to be over an hour's drive northeast of Dodge when she checked online and was secluded in the countryside.

Up and down forest lined winding roads the car went as she looked at a few places with open land, but didn't see any other businesses, only a few houses, or farms, mostly just trees and fields.

Along the way there were Private Property signs posted, but the road was open to the public, but had very little traffic. Then up ahead she saw a fenced in compound and complex comprised of numerous buildings, a fence, a gate and a huge sign and big letters that said, RIM, which she remembered stood for Responsive Integrated Machines.

This must be the place, she thought, and approached the security gate, stopped and rolled down her window. As she waved, said, hello to a guard who came out.

He was armed which made her feel a bit of tension, and he was holding a computer tablet. A few more guards looked her way through the large glass window of the building at the gate.

"Yes, can I help you?" the guard said.

"My name is Sue Kick, and here to see my father, Otto Vortich. I'm supposed to meet him here this morning."

The guard looked at his tablet. "Yes, and you're Sue Kick?"

"Yes, that's me."

"We have to check everyone who enters the complex. Can I see your I.D., or driver's license?"

"Sure, here you go," she said, and handed her license to the guard.

The guard looked at it, then at her. "Your first time here?" he asked.

"Yes, it is."

The guard gave the license back and entered some information into a tablet computer. "Here's a pass to wear while you're on the site. You can park your car over there," the guard pointed to a fenced in area.

"That's the parking for visitors. and this card goes on the dash of your car. Just make sure it's visible, so they know you're here with a pass. I was told someone will come to meet and pick you up. You can just wait in or by your car for them. Have a good day, miss."

"Okay, thanks," Sue said, and followed the guard's instructions, driving slowly to the parking area and parking in one of the open spaces. She turned off the engine, rolled up the window, grabbed her bag and waited in front of her car.

After a few minutes her attention focused on a woman dressed in a suit who slowly approached. She was slender, tall, wearing black pants, jacket and trendyshoes. Her white shirt had a flared collar, and was undone at the top.

She extended her hand. "Hello, Sue, I'm Gabriella, but everyone calls me, Gabby."

I wonder where's she's from, Sue thought as she listened to the woman's accent. "Hi, I'm Sue." *She sounds like she's from a country in Europe.*

"I've heard a little about you from your father, and how you have rekindled your relationship after such a long period of time. I think it's just wonderful how you guys were able to get together."

"Yes, we're getting to know each other day by day."

"Well, it's a nice day for you to visit. Did you have a nice drive here?"

"I'm a little overwhelmed at how big this place is, surprised actually. Also that it's in the countryside;

there's nothing else around here."

"Yes, it is a large facility," Gabby said. "Your dad bought all of this land years ago from local farmers. Do you have your bag and everything you need to take along? You know you don't have to worry about anything. You can leave your things in the car if you wish. It'll be safe."

"Okay," Sue said. "I'll just take my bag then. Don't really need aything else."

"Then, follow me," Gabby said. "We'll go this way."

"How long have you worked here?" Sue asked as she followed Gabby.

"Been here from the time this place was built," Gabby said. "I've put in a lot of hours, and forgotten how many years now that I've been here."

"You enjoy working for my father's company."

"Yes, it's a very exciting place to work at, and this is a special time to be here doing it. AI and tech is advancing like crazy," Gabby said. "I think you'll feel that way too after seeing some things we are doing here today. We're truely working on beyond cutting edge technology, and ahead of of just about every other company in this field. So, just to let you know, Mr. Vortich is not here at the moment, so I'll show you around for a while until he gets back, should be arriving soon though. Let's go this way."

They walked through the entrance, a tinted glass wall from the ground to the top. Gabby took out her ID card and waved it in front of the security scanner.

"You guys have pretty tight security around here," Sue said. "Are you working on some secret projects?"

"Yes, actually, security is tight, but this card is typically used by all employees and visitors. Some areas use facial or fingerprint, and the higher a person goes in the company the more security. There are confidential issues, some contracts are for the government, so I can't really talk about it in too much detail, but can show you a few things that might surprise you. Let's take this elevator."

"Michael was offered a job, but he's not interested in working here because he really likes what he does."

"He builds thing I've heard," Gabby said. "Works with stone? Maybe we could offer him some work? We're always building, changing things around, and we need someone who can handel complicated construction projects."

"Yes, that's right," Sue said. "How did you hear he's a builder?"

"Oh," she said, "from Mr. Vortich. He mentioned that Michael might be interested in working here, and tried hard by offering him a great package, but Michael said he enjoyed building things."

"Learned his craft from his grandfather, and started when he was just a kid. It's a small business, usually just a two man crew, occasionally hires from around town. They're guys who hang out at the bar, and can do the work relatively well. He's helping them out because they need some quick cash."

"Well, if he changes his mind, he's always welcome to join the company. I'm sure Mr. Vortich would hire him in no time. You could work her, too. Have you thought about that? It's interesting work I think. You might like it."

"No, not really," I'm like Michael in a way, that I don't have any advanced IT skills."

"You could learn," Gabby said, then the elevator stopped, and they walked through another secure area to be checked by the security system.

"This is the robotics section." The room was big, there were shelves to the ceiling, had computers and monitors scattered around the room. She pointed across the room. "This guy over here is quite amazing. Let me show you what he can do."

A full sized robot stood, perched on top of a 3ft x 3ft x 3ft silver cube on the other side of the room it moved and stood at attention like soldier.

Five of these cubes on the floor were in line, spaced apart, straight in a row. Gabby picked up a small controller, and pointed it at the robot. It jumped across to the next box, and continued all the way across jumping on the cubes, then turned around, and started back to the other side. It stopped halfway, then did a back flip back to the cube where it started from.

"I've never seen any thing like that before," Sue said. "It's amazing."

"We call him Jack after the Rolling Stones song. Let's run it one more time." She pointed the controller at Jack and it went through the same routine, jumping across the boxes perfectly like an acrobat.

"Wow!" Sue said. "I still can't believe how it can jump, and do back flips. What's it going to be used for?"

"We're thinking of possible applications for it, military, security, some dangerous situations like fires, or other disasters. Let's go to another room. Follow me."

"This is where we're working on AR, and AI. If you put this glasses on you'll be able to see some crazy things flying and moving around in the room." Gabby handed the glasses to Sue, and helped her adjust the fit.

"Are you ready?"

"I'm ready," Sue said.

"Here we go," Gabby said, and pushed some buttons on a control panel, the floor turned into water, and a whale jumped up, and dove back in.

"What do you think?"

"It looks so real," Sue said. "What else is there?" Then a dragon dropped from the ceiling after it turned to look like the sky. It flew around the room, and back up through the ceiling.

"It's really fantastic, isn't it? Your father's the developer of all of this, and it's only the beginning of what can be, but I can't get into that too much more right now. You can find out more after you've talked to him."

"I can't imagine how any of this happens or how it could be improved," Sue said.

"I'll take to your father's office now," Gabby said. "He should be back soon, and show you around more a little later."

They stood in front of the elevator that went to the top floor of the highest building in the compound. "I'm afraid you're on your own now, Sue. I can't go up with because I don't have the clearance for that area. This elevator goes directly to your father's office, and he said it was programmed to take you up. So, I'll talk to you later, it was so nice to meet you."

"Thanks for showing me around," Sue said. "I'm overwhelmed by this place."

The elevator doors closed, they waved, and Sue was on her way up, and then the doors opened to a spacious classic looking room seeming to be void of any technology. A solid wooden desk in view with bookshelves from floor to ceiling covering both walls on either side with a huge colorful rug fixed in the center of the room. Sue walked to the desk, her hand rested on top caressing the wood from edged to edge.

Then she noticed the dark brown leather throne of a chair behind the desk, and made her way around to have a closer look. On the desk she glanced at the leather bound gold trimmed album with the name VORTICH embossed in the middle. She opened the cover, looked at the first page and the inscription or title read -THE GOLDEN DAWN-

Sue blinked and was about to turn the page again, but the room changed, and now it was a modern industrial looking space. "What the . . . happened?" she whispered. "What was that?" then the elevator doors opened. She looked up and smiled. "Hello," she said a moment later.

Otto, her father, the father that she had been reunited with had stepped out of the elevator smiling. "Hi, Sue!" he approached the desk, and they met in the middle of the room. "I'm sorry I kept you, had some things to take care of, but I'm here now."

"You've go an interesting office."

"You like it? It's changing all the time, but I've got everything I need here. Are you hungry?"
"Yeah, a little."

"Let's go to the cafeteria, and after that I can show you around a little more."

"Gabby showed me a bit all ready, but this place is so big, I had no idea of it's size."

"It's grown over the years, and still expanding. I've purchased all of the the surrounding land to build on."

"It's really overwhelming," she said. "I'd like to see more. I asked Michael to come, but he's busy building something with Moses."

"I'll keep asking him if he would like to take a position here, but Sue, are you interested in working here? I wasn't sure you would be, so hadn't mentioned it. I think it would be very interesting for you, and after finding your way around could work on whatever you'd like, basically pick your own projects."

"Sounds like a dream job."

"It could be for you, think about it," Otto said. "There's the cafe over there." They grabbed some food and sat at a table near a window.

"I'm still trying to wrap my head around all of this. I can't imagine what will come of it."

"Let me ask you a question, Sue."

"Okay."

"What if you were lost in a place, a forest or desert, and came upon a helicopter, could you fly it?"
"Probably not," she said.

"Now wait," Otto said. "What if you had the skill to fly it, but it wouldn't start, and you had to fix it. Could you do that?"

"I can't even fly it, so how could I repair it? Is this a job interview?"

Otto laughed, then said. "Well I have asked questions like that in interviews. It's related to problem solving, and solving them is connected to involvement. There may be no reason for being, except for human need to solve them."

Then his phone rang. "Sorry Sue, but I've got to take care of something."

"Another problem?" she asked, and laughed."

"Yes," he smiled, and said. "Some people are blind and can't see the solutions even when they're right in front of them. Why don't you go back to my office and I'll meet you there."

"Okay, I'd like to see more," Sue said.

"Here's a card pass to take the elevator to my office," Otto said.

"Once you're in the office check out the computer on my desk. There's information about the company that you can read. I'll call you after I take care of this issue, which I'm sure is really nothing, be right back."

EXPLORING THE VAULT

Sue got into the same elevator she'd been in previously to go up to her father's office. Again the doors closed, but there was no movement up or down as she was engulfed in silence. Then a humming sound grew with intensity and startled her after she pushed the button for the first floor. Now she felt movement, the elevator jerked upward and downward.

She reached for the controls, slamming as many different floor numbers as humanly possible, but it dropped downward with certainty faster and faster. Her vision blurred creating cloudy thoughts, she felt dizzy almost the same as being a on a merry-go-round, then lost consciousness.

She woke sprawled out on the elevator floor looking up at the ceiling wondering where she was, feeling a touch of fear with no memory whatsoever, like first birth entering into a new world surrounded by darkness flowing from inside onto a bright expanding blank canvas.

How much time has gone by?

Questions rose in her mind on being human, and purpose of life crossed her mind as she felt a shadow engulf her. A feeling on her face carried a vision of strength physical and mental, along with ideas, but emotions without control, forcing her into a state of a dream world.

Sue stood looking into the deep dark black space leading to a tunnel with no end in sight. First she felt fear, then thoughts of problem solving, and how to figure out this particular one energized her. She looked at the stone floor, and examined how the bricks were arranged in a herringbone pattern.

The ceiling was laced in a basket weave of stone rope pattern, the walls a running flowing tight bond moving continuously around a circumference. She noticed her clothes were different, but had no memory of changing, and now a sleek tight soft dark gray skin like material covered her body.

Out of the blue a woman's voice echoed, "I'm here Sue, and been waiting for you."

Sue looked around, but saw no one. "Who are you? Where are you?"

"I'm your friend, and here to help you with your journey."

"You say you're here, but I don't see you. And help me? Just how will you help me? And where am I going? Where is this journey taking me?"

"I'm here to find your way and to help manifest the purpose of your existence. I know you've recently found and reunited with your parents, and you're trying to figure out who they are, and why they befriended you after such a long time."

"You're going to tell me, or show me how to do that?"

"I'm going to tell you why and what you can do," the voice said.

"I'm going to show you reality to another dimension, talk about ideas that you have thought about, but never acted on."

Sue walked slowly following a light that became brighter, and the stone walls on either side were taking changing shape. She saw figures and symbols scratched randomly into the walls. "What do those markings mean?"

"They tell a story," the voice said, "and we're going to add your story to the wall. You will do things that you thought impossible or never imagined, and make your imprint on history."

"What is my story, and my history?"

"It can be anything you can imagine; that's how this life works in this place. You make your journey as you see it, and paint your life's picture on the canvas of eternity."

"I've thought of myself as a painter, but have never really painted anything that I felt was great, have done some sketches, and gotten good feedback from people. Can you give me a little more detail on the canvas of eternity?"

"This canvas is more than just a normal painting. I'm talking about a canvas of earth, sky, sun, moon, the solar system, and the unseen micro and macro world. You can make it however you want, whatever you want, and become whoever you want."

"How is that possible? I can't comprehend any of what you're describing."

"You keep walking, the light will shine, shadows will form, and your thoughts will make the world you imagine."

"Why can't you tell me exactly who you are or where you come from?"

"I can only say that I'm a voice, a friend, a guide, but you can make me into whatever you like, and this will continue until what happens last."

"And what happens last?"

"After everything else is finished, and you have no other alternatives, I will pass on knowledge that will help you to start again. This is a stage you cannot understand until you actually experience the point of no turning back. Your friend Michael knows this singular time because he has gone though it many times, but for some reason can't take the final step."

"You know Michael? How?"

"I've watched him from the old time."

"Old time? What's old time?"

"It's when there was no time as you know, we can't even say time before time, it was the time of Rim Stone."

"What's Rim Stone?"

"I have said too much, you're not ready for this yet."

"How will I know when I'm ready, and when to start the cycle again? Are you the only one who knows this, and when it happens? Will I know later?"

"I've said too much."

The walls began to fade, and the surrounding field of vision turned into a forest of trees, hills and trails that looked familiar. The dirt path below was covered with broken sticks, and sounds of birds echoing in the air came into sight in the blue sky, and magical clouds shapes floated overhead. Sue walked toward the sound of a train that rumbled in the distance, and as she watched from the top of cliff, it disappeared from the horizon.

"I know this place," Sue said. "Hello." There was no answer from the voice. "Hello," she said again, than louder with an echo fading,

"Hello!"

She turned and walked unguided knowing exactly where to go, making her way through a perfectly cut tunnel following a path down to the water. *How do I know where to go? I don't remember ever being in this place.* She stood there looking out over the water flowing by remembering anything that popped into her mind.

She closed her eyes, an image of Michael swimming out to a body floating out in the middle of a steadily flowing river. *How did I get here? Didn't this happen years ago?* "I'm just outside Hungry Point," she whispered.

She was familiar with the area and woods, and turned to make her way to the cabin. Along as she walked down the trail in the woods images appeared, she turned following the path she'd been on many times, and more images of people and events flashed in front of her.

"What is going on? How can this be?" *Why is it happening again?*
Sue walked out from the edge of the trees and the cabin she had spent time at came into focus. On the deck sitting on the bench was Michael's grandfather, Poppy. She recognized him and waved, he stood, and walked into the cabin without seeing noticing her. As she approached the cabin it seemed to fade, and when she stopped it came back in focus.

What is happening?

Measuring her movement forward step by step she got closer, but as before the cabin faded, then as her shoe touched the first step on the deck of the cabin it was gone, only trees and sky remained. At the edge of the forest an older man stood watching, then beckoned. Sue walked toward him, but her vision blurred as it did when this journey started. She collapsed, fell to the ground, and when her eyes opened she was on floor in her father's office.

She picked herself off the floor still weak braced firmly on the desk.
There was a flask of water there, so she poured some into a glass, drank, and when she put it down the elevator doors opened.

Otto stood there and saw Sue wobbly, then dashed toward the desk, grabbing and holding her from falling again. "Are you okay," he asked, and saw glazed eyes, her limp body. "Sue?" he helped her to the sofa, then brought her some water. "Drink this."

After drinking the water she sat up. "Hello, she said.

"What happened? Are you okay? Should I call our health staff?"

"I don't know what happened. Maybe it was something I had to eat at the cafe."

"I had the same food and I'm fine," Otto said. "Just rest here, maybe we can schedule another day to see more of the compound. Can you can drive or would like me to have someone drive you home?"

"I should be fine," she said. "I'm feeling better already." She stood, and stretched like she'd just woken from a nap. I had a dream, and I'm started to remember it."

"What do you remember from the dream?"

"I came in here and the room got blurry. No, wait, I was in the elevator and going down so fast I couldn't see straight, and ended up in a tunnel with stone walls that turned into trees, then I was at Michael's cabin." aaaaaaaaaaaa"Sounds pretty normal to me for a dream," Otto said. "I've never seen this cabin, it sounds like a nice place, and you seem attached to it."

"I'll take you there someday, and we can have a barbecue."

"Sure, sounds, Sue. Are you sure that you can drive home?"

"Yeah, I'm fine. Don't worry."

"I have to worry, it's part of being your father. I'll walk you down to your car whenever you're ready."

After a bit rest Sue and Otto took the elevator down, and he walked her to the parking lot. She started the car and drove out through the gate, and nodded to the guards. As Otto watched Sue drive away with a satisfied expression he turned and smiled at Gabby.

"Your daughter is very nice Mr. Vortrich. Will she be coming back?"

"Oh, yes, she'll be back," Otto said. "She very interested in working here, and maybe you can be her mentor. How would that be?"

"Sure, I'd be happy to help out. What will she be doing here?"

"I'm sure we'll be able to keep her busy, and she'll know what to do after she starts working here."

"I guess there's always something to do, and she does seem very interested."

"Oh, yes," Otto said. "I'm really glad how things arte working out."

THE LIQUOR SALESMAN

Sue was at Kick's bar cleaning the store room, and during this time, she came across a box of old photographs. While looking through the photo albums she found a dusty envelope filled with poems.

Either someone from the family, a relative, or a friend, must have written these, she thought.

She opened one album and most of the pictures were faded, so even though she tried to figure out some of the faces in the pictures, couldn't clearly make out any of the people or kids. It was as if all the people were just close relatives and friends, but also strangers or people she'd never known or ever met.

I wonder who these people are, where they are now, what they're doing now.

From the title of the poem on the first page she knew the poem was about wine, and while reading it to herself, thought the words seemed familiar, and a connection to events in the past.

APOCOPE

Up along the trellis no longer touching earth

A cheerful crawling vine twisting all around

Every which way and that this color of pine

Destination unknown, ornamental tangle of ribbon

Shift course, new virgin line hunting sunlight and rain

Roots grow robust, leaver bluster and shine

Climate a struggle, what yield to come

We pray it be fine, harvest stage, amine

Interlude for the throng, celebrating bounty

Jubilee . . . drink sweet wine!

From stories she heard growing up she knew her step dad and grandfather had the same name, J. Kick. The way people kept their names straight, and who they were addressing was to call the elder, J. Kick, and junior just Kick. She also heard stories and saw pictures of granddad J. Kick who she understood was a liquor salesman, and traveled from town to town selling liquor, and eventually saved enough money to open a bar called, Outsiders Inn, what is still the one and only bar in Hungry Point. Since he was in the liquor business, and the poems were about food and drink, Sue thought that maybe he wrote the poems about wine and other topics.

Another story shared and retold happened in the winter when a few years after opening the bar, granddad J. Kick dissapeared without a trace. There was a quasi investigation by local police, and they concluded the incident was a deer hunting accident. J. Kick had gone off hunting alone when he vanished, and there were no witnesses. Because all of the evidence seemed to lead in a the way of a hunting accident, his son of the same name took over the bar from then on.

Some years after the death of his father and taking over the operation, Kick found a baby one night in the bar at closing time. This event was talked about in Hungry Point for a long time because like most small towns, days in Hungry Point were typically unchanging except for a few, and that one night after closing time when Kick made the surprising discovery.

The story going around town was that as Kick did his nightly clean-up routine at the bar one night, heard a noise coming from under one of the tables, and this caught his attention as it sounded like an animal cry. So, thinking an animal had strayed into the bar he grabbed the baseball bat kept behind the bar. He kept it there for rowdy customers who had drunk too much, and wanted to convince them to leave or severe damage would be inflicted. Kick, being an impressive figure, only had to slam it on the bar, and that would take of any thoughts of further argument.

But this time and moment caught him off guard, so with great surprise his heart melted that late night because he found a baby crying in what looked like a picnic basket under a table and clueless how it had arrived there.

On occasion during a night out drinking someone would leave an item at the bar and usually show up the next day to claim said item. Kick determined that two or three days should be long enough for someone to discover their misplaced their belongings. If the items were not claimed they were put in the back room. But a baby, well that was a first. Never had anyone left a child in the bar, and he couldn't just put the baby in the back room, so he contacted a friend he thought could help, then later the authorities.

A police officer and representative from the orphanage in Dodge drove to Hungry Point to visit Kick. By then Kick had taken the baby home and cared for it as best he could. A friend he knew with small children provided help with basic supplies until the baby could be picked up, and cared for long term.

There was a knock on the door; Kick opened it holding the baby in his arms as a police officer, and care-giver from the orphanage stood there smiling seeing this unusual situation.

"Evening Mr. Kick," the police offer said. "We're here to pick up the baby."

"Hi," Kick said. "Thanks for coming, it's been pretty hectic here since I found her at the bar. Come on in. She hasn't been too much trouble. I'm actually getting attached to her."

"Well, I can't remember ever hearing a baby being left at a bar," the police officer said as he looked at her. "She's cute alright."

Kick handed the cute warm bundle to the social worker. "What will happen to her? Where are you taking her?"

"We'll try to locate the parents through our parent network," the social worker said. "If we can't she'll be put up for adoption. In cases like this I doubt we'll be able locate her parents because of the way she was left on her own."

"How long will you look for her parents?"

"We never stop looking, but the intensity slows when we realize or think no one is coming. You know how it goes; people aren't interested in getting involved. And kids get older as well."

"Can anyone adopt her," Kick asked. "How does the process work anyway?"

"Basically, we try to place a child with a couple that can't or have no kids, and a baby is what most of them want. People think it's easier to raise a baby as your own child other than a teenager."

"Can I hold her again," Kick said. "She's so cute."

"Well, that's about it," the police officer said, and Kick handed the baby to the social worker.

"What if a single person wanted to adopt her? Is that possible?"

"I guess it's possible, but it just doesn't usually occur," the social worker said. "I've never personally handled a case like that, but doesn't mean it couldn't happen, depends on the circumstances and other factors."

"But it's possible?" Kick asked.

"Technically, I guess so, but highly unlikely because we look to place children with two-parent households."

"Where are you taking her now?"

"She'll be taken to the orphanage in Dodge," the social worker said.

"She'll stay there, and if the birth parents come in we'll go through the process to check them out, and make sure they're responsible. Because of what happened, and how the child was found, the threshold to return the child is high."

"How responsible can they be if the left her at a bar? I don't see how that could even be considered."

"Right, we'll be looking into everything, and there are people on the waiting list, but the process takes six months to a year."

"What's the first step to adoption?"

"The first step is the application and fee."

"Fee?" Kick said. "There's always money involved. Guess everything costs something, and we have to pay someone to do the paperwork. Then what happens, after the fee is paid?"

"A profile packet is filled out, a home study is done, development stage, activation and recognition as guardian. Of course that's a rudimentary short answer to your question, there's more to it, and there would be follow up visits. Are you interested in adopting her?"

"Well, you know, I get the feeling she was left at my bar for a reason," Kick said. "I don't know the reason, but sure there's one."

"All I can say is come to the orphanage, then we can start the process," the social worker said. "We'll take it one step at a time."

"Okay," Kick said. "I'll be there tomorrow."

"You are serious about this aren't you?"

"Yes, I am, and believe I can take good care of her."

"She'll be in good hands until then, Mr. Kick, don't worry."

Kick watched them get into the car, then waved as they left, then got choked up, and wiped a tear from his cheek. *Don't worry little one, I'm coming to get you.*

As the car drove on the country road back to Dodge the baby slept while the police officer and social worker got to know each other.

"You been with the orphanage a long time?" the police officer asked.

"No, Just started working there," the social worker said. "I'm an orphan myself, and luckily adopted by a well-to-do couple, so my life changed completely. I realized that it was my social responsibility to help other kids like me."

"That's quite a story, and wonderful of you to give back. You must really like this kind of work, then?"

"It's okay up to now," she said, "but of course it's hard when really small children are involved. I'm just trying to help."

"How about you?" she asked, "been with the police department a while?"

"Yeah, I've been with them about ten years now."

"What made you get into law enforcement?"

"I guess like you I was interested in helping people, especially people who aren't able to help themselves."

"Have you ever had to use your gun?"

"Put my hand on it, but never had to pull it out on

duty, only for target practice. Have you ever gotten into any difficult situations with families you've been involved with?"

"So far so good, they've all been pretty typical situations. Well, as typical as can be because I'm dealing with adoptions."

"Are you free tonight? What are you doing for dinner tonight?"

"No plans. Why?"
"Just wondering if you'd be interested in having dinner with me?"

"Sure, love to, where are we going?"

"I was thinking about steak house in Dodge, they have pretty good food."

"What time is good for you?"

"How about seven?"

"Perfect, I'll pick you up at six-thirty."

***

The adoption was not an easy feat, but finally Kick convinced the court that this was God's divine providence and meant to be his responsibility to raise the child. With help from friends the child flourished and grew to be beautiful woman. Kick named her Sue; a take on the Johnny Cash song, and legally gave her his family name Kick.

So, in the end Kick arranged to adopt the child, and raised her as his own daughter. As far as she knew Kick was her dad, but there were questions about her mother, and Kick couldn't answer any of them when asked.

After Sue was older, and could understand the situation, Kick told her what had happened. How he had found her under the table in the bar one night after closing time. Sue had come to believe that her real parents were not interested in her life, or had passed away by now, so from that time on she considered Kick to be her dad.

Living with Kick she learned fishing, hunting, camping, and spent a lot of time with the Colts. Michael especially because Kick and Poppi were close friends, and both of them liked the outdoors. Poppi did some work for Kick, fixing and renovating the bar, and built a huge stone fireplace in the bar which became an attraction in its own right, and kind of a way for Poppi to promote his mason work and business. Sue and Michael started to spend more time with each other's family, more time together by themselves, and soon they were inseparable soul mates.

Then one day when Sue and Michael were on a camping trip, Poppi's truck was discovered burning in the back of the cabin by his partner Moses. There was nothing Moses could do because by the time he'd arrived, the truck was engulfed in flames. In the police report they said he died in the fire, but Michael always felt there was something strange about what had happened to Poppi. He felt there to be gaps in time because he'd never known Poppi, or seen him looking any differently, so in his mind Michael thought something just wasn't right. Michael always had those thoughts in mind as he got older.

The news reports of the day said that there had been hurricane strength winds only in Hungry Point that day. Along with the wind, reports of an endless peculiar bell like sound echoed through the area. On the day of Poppi's funeral Michael couldn't get out of bed. He lay there in a semi coma mumbling in a language no one, not even he, understood, and the next day had no recollection of it happening.

Poppi and Moses had worked together for a number of years building stone walls and fireplaces, so he took over the business, and Michael worked with Moses. Michael learned about being a stone mason quickly as if he'd always had the knowledge within himself. He eventually took over, and did most of the work as Moses grew old.

UNIVERSITY DAYS

The campus was fairly large for a Midwestern town nestled between the Mississippi, Wisconsin, and Black rivers. The town is Lacrosse, and the story goes the name comes from French explorers who saw the Natives play, *The little Brother of War*, a game to practice and simulate battle. The stick they used to play the game looked like a French Bishop's staff called a Crozier. The town's name also could have something to do with the crossing of rivers where fur trading took place.

A New Yorker, Nathan Myrick, settled in the area and opened a trading post near where the rivers met, and to this day there's a park with his name. Because of the broad plain, tall bluffs, and good river access, this was an ideal location for trade and development.

Also to the east is a scenic vista, Grand Dad bluff, which overlooks the sprawling and long river valley. Once the railroad spur was built the area grew quickly becoming a center for the growing lumber industry, followed by beer brewing, and other manufacturing of the time.

Winter is brutal in Wisconsin; temperatures can drop to lows of minus 50, and thinking back I wonder how anyone was ever able to survive. I can't imagine living there without the modern conveniences available today. Sliding down hills of snow in winter is enjoyable for kids, but cold wind builds drifts across the roads make it tough to travel anywhere, and ice cycles hang from the eves of houses gleaming when the sun makes an appearance. Spring is wet, cool, and dew attached to the grass in the morning flickers like a blanket of diamonds.

Summer is a mix of sunshine, occasionally humid, also the best time for camping on the Mississippi River. Autumn is pleasant and fights winter, but eventually yields and winter is the winner, then there are fewer pleasant days and the frozen time begins. The cycle continues, starts over, changes year to year, and special for one reason or another.

There's a cemetery filled with a variety of engraved tombstones across the street from the campus, and next to it a park with trees, bungalows for parties, barbecues, a football field, dormitories, library, halls, auditoriums, and a cafeteria. Some students live off campus with roommates in houses that investors buy for the sole purpose of renting them out to students.

From my dreams and memories I recall being there to study architecture. I walked to the campus every morning passing by the football field and dormitories. Occasionally a speaker would come to share a message on various topics from business, politics, and once a man came to give a talk on dreams, dimensions, and how stories and history are passed down throughout time.

The place where I lived was an older house with enough rooms for five students who shared the kitchen, living room, and it had a small back yard. My room was upstairs facing a narrow back alley with a gravel road. There was a small shed for yard tools, a place to park bikes, where trash cans were located, a grill to barbecue and keep some lawn furniture for sitting outside in nice weather. It took about fifteen minutes to walk to class and five by bike. All of the houses in the neighborhood around the campus were all occupied by students.

After moving there Michael used to work on his car in the street, and one time while installing an audio system, and connecting wires under the dash, had a memorable experience. The car door was open, his head under the dash, feet outside touching the ground next to the curb on the passenger side, all while holding a light under the dash and connecting stereo wires.

He couldn't see, but felt hands rubbing his stomach and crotch. After he sqirmed his way out, it turned out to be the girl who lived next door. She had short red hair, wore bluejean bib oveall shorts, and could talk up a storm. On that particular day she was bored and had nothing to do. During their conversation he discovered she was a masseuse, and the afternoon that day was pleasant.

Enjoyment came from helping his grandfather. Poppi liked teaching Michael, and at bedtime when he was a kid, Poppi told Michael stories. Some stories were about military operations, and a special agent who always got away saving the day. Then later at an older age he shared stories on how Michael's parents were killed in a car accident, and this was the reason for living with him. After hearing the story a number of times certain details seemed to change.

Poppi had been in the military, his son as well, and how Michael's dad met his mother. Poppi had photo albums of Michael's parents when they lived in Austria, where he had been stationed before they moved to a family farm that belonged to Poppi's older brother. He helped with the chores on the farm until deciding what he would do after the service, and that was when the car accident happened. At least what he was told by Poppi. He was little at the time,and had no memory of any time spent with his parents, except for the dreams about flying in an airplane. And that's how or why he ended up staying and living with Poppi.

Of course all of this seemed to make sense to him, but anything can be processed and formulated to add up, that's the beauty of numbers, dates, and ideas. On occasion for an unexplainable reason he felt like he'd come from some far away place. He enjoyed looking up to sky, watching the stars, closing his eyes and imagined floating in space. Slowly through the stories Poppi told, and through the people in them, he became to realize there was a much larger story about life in this world as we understand.

Curiosity grew at school when by coincidence Michael decided to take a class called Psychological Physics thinking it would help in studying architecture. The course included, a Set Operator Measure Game, Lattice and Ergodic Theory, along with Mathematical Economics Statistics, Fluid Dynamics, and Cognitive Abilities. He had little understanding of most of this, but felt drawn and compelled to take the class after seeing the name of the professor teaching it posted on the schedule.

He remembered the first day of the class, how the professor of the class spoke with what sounded like a French accent, and also on that day felt that they had met him somewhere previously. The professor began the class explaining what he was going to cover, and that if there were ever any questions we should ask because he was there to help. Signed up for the class were about thirty students from a wide range of backgrounds.

There was one student who seemed to be watching Michael, or gave off that impression, so he wondered who he was because he thought he'd met him before too. This student sat quietly not saying much, just writing in his notebook, and this kept Michael thinking about why he had these feelings.

After the class Michael just couldn't get the professor off of his mind. From the way he moved and spoke, he felt down deep this was not the first time they had met, so after the class he followed him to his office. He was basically finished for the day and had no plans for the rest of the afternoon. Michael knocked on the door, it opened, and there stood the professor.

"Yes, what can I do for you?"

"Hello, well . . . ." he mumbled not knowing what to say. "Could I talk to you for a few minutes Professor Paris?"

"Sure," he said. "Come in and have a seat." The office had a large wooden desk covered with books and papers. There was fairly large window to the left, and a couple of tall shelves on the right. Light from the window painted the room with an afternoon golden glow, and there was the lingering aroma of patchouli oil. He gestured for Michael to sit, so he walked closer, sat in the wooden chair in front of his desk. Paris went behind, and sat in his large black leather chair. He closed a book, moved it to the side, then put his elbows on the desk and leaned forward.

"How can I help you, Michael?"

"You know my name," he said. "I'm surprised."

"Well, I like to know who's taking my class," Paris said.

Michael took a deep breath. "I don't want you to take this the wrong way, and you can throw me out of you office, but I've got to ask. Have we met before?"

He let out a hearty laughed. "Why do you think we've met before?"

"I can't say why," he said. "It's just a gut feeling I have."
Paris sat back in his chair, both of them looking at and watching each other for a time. "Why did you sign up for my class?"

"I don't know," Michael said. "I guess I thought it would help me be a better architect."

"You like designing and building things?"

"Yes, I learned from my grandfather. he taught me about masonry, and I've always been interested how patterns are made with materials, and especially with stone."

"Your grandfather," Paris said, "not your father?"

"I never really knew my father. He died when I was very young, and I have no memories of him or my mother."

"No memory at all? What did your grandfather tell you about your parents?"

"That they were killed in a car accident."

"I belive that certain people have information that others do not."

"I'm sorry I don't understand what you're saying."

"Of course you wouldn't now. What I'm going to show you, and what we say from now on stays between us, agree?"

"Sure, agree."

"What if I told you most people are totally in the dark about how they think of the world. And known history is only a small part of the story of why things are the way they are."

"You mean there's some secret that people don't know?"

"Not some secret, but the secret."

"What secret? Can you tell me?"

"Come here tomorrow after class, and I'll tell you more. That's all I want to tell you for now. This is information that I can't let out to just anyone."

"Michael stood, extended his hand to the professor, and they held a tight grip. Michael turned to leave, but stopped a moment. "We have met before, I know it. I think I'm beginning to understand why I feel this way."

The next day after class Michael headed to the professor's office, and noticed on the way that the student who had eyed him in class was shadowing his movements. *Why is this guy following me?*

Michael walked in different directions, went into buildings, up elevators, down stairs, and felt comfortable he had gotten away from the student who was following him. Michael knocked on the professor's door.

"Hello, Michael, come in."

"I've got to tell you that a student from class followed me here. I think he's been following me a lot, and I feel know him in a kind of way, like I know you, but not sure why. Like I said, he always seems to be watching me in class for some reason, and after class he shows up in places where I go."

"It's okay let's not worry about him now. Sit down."

"We shouldn't worry about it?"

"I didn't say not to worry, but let's not think about it now."

"Okay, whatever you say, Professor," Michael said, and looked around the office again, taking notice of the books on the shelves.
The professor smiled, grabbed a piece of paper and drew a shape, then showed it to Michael. "What do you think of this? Have you ever seen anything like this before?"

"Yes, I know that shape, and wear a similar design around my neck." He reached down into the collar of his shirt, and pulled out a pendant he'd been given by his grandfather, Poppi. As usual ,as he held it in his hand it warmed, and seemed to fill with energy. It was a simple drawing, and the same design of the pendant. How do you know about it?"

"Put it away," he said.

Michael followed his instructions. "How do you know about it?"

"I'm the one who designed it," he said. "And we have met, well in a way. Let's just say in a previous time before you were you."

"What do you mean? That makes no sense."

"It makes perfect sense to me, and will to you soon. Why are you here at this school, and why did you sign up for my class?"

"I don't really know," he said. "I thought I could learn something about architecture. There is some relation to what you're teaching and this design."

"Okay, in my class we'll study how to build things in the world, of the universe, and what's in it. Is that what you want?"

"Yes, but I want to know more," he said. "I know there's more to this than building things."

"Yes, that's true, there is more to learn and know. We'll start after the next class, and go one step at a time from here on out. This will all take a bit of time to absorb, there's so much information, and we have to be careful."

"Why do we need to be careful?" Michael asked.

"Careful of that student following especially, because I think he wants what you've got."

"He wants my pendant?"

"Yes, so keep it under wraps, and don't tell anyone else about it."

"Okay, thank you, for your help," Michael said, then walked out of the professor's office with an open mind, and longing to know something more, but not sure what or why.

Leaving the building Michael became more aware of his surroundings. He was more careful how he walked around campus, and back to his apartment.

The student who followed him appeared in front of the professor's building after Michael had left. He waited there seemingly for the professor, and when Paris stepped out and walked to the parking lot was followed by the student. After the professor got into his car the student stood behind the car so he couldn't back up.After looking in the rear view mirror, rolled down his window, turned to the back and motioned for the student to come over. He stood there not moving, then turned and walked away.

***

FIRST PRINCIPLE

"Look at this, Michael," Sue said, "there's an article here in the paper about a guy describing the First Principle theory. I think I remember you talking about it a while ago. Do you remember? Didn't you tell me about it when we were camping on the river once? Something about a teacher you had I think.

We were looking at the stars, finding constellations, meaningful patterns of mythological creatures that date way beyond our comprehension, all while trying to figure how theses concepts came into existence."

"That's pretty good. You sound like you know what you're talking about. Maybe you give that class."

"Actually that's what it says here in the article. I'm just

reading it"

"What exactly does the article say it say? Who is the guy? Is there a name? When is this happening?"

"According what it says in the paper he's speaking at the university in Dodge this Friday night. Want to go? I'll tag along. Why were you interested in first principle anyway?"

"What's the guy's name?"

"Let's see," Sue said, "here's his name. It says, Professor Luke Paris. Have you heard of him? Do you know the name?"

"Yeah, that's the guy I read about," Michael said. "This is great, perfect. What time does he start talking?"

"Says it starts at seven pm."

"Do we need to tickets, have to make a reservation or anything?"

"Don't see anything about booking here, and I think it's free."

"Free? Really? Let's see that." Sue handed the paper to Michael and pointed to the article. "Here it is, right here on this page."

"Yeah, you're right, nothing about cost. Guess it is free. I want to go. You're coming with me, right? I think you'll find it interesting."

"I'll go, but you'll have to fill me in on the details because I'm not sure what all this really means. I only know what you've been talking about."

"I'm not really clear on what any of this or what it all really means, but ask me anything you like, and I'll try to give you the answer if I can. We should know more and be somewhat clear after we hear him give his talk. I've got a good feeling about it."
"I guess if you've got a good feeling about that's all I need to know."

The man speaking at the university campus in Dodge on First Principle theory had given Michael some ideas on how to develop and think in a different way. It was not just outside the box, but a belief that there is no box, actually that the world as we know it is only a only a small piece of everything that's happening.

There isn't even a name for what it's called as far as he knew, only that anything imaginable is possible. A deep understanding of drilling down to the basic foundation of an idea, and to start at the very beginning, the first step or what comes before the first step. An assumption that cannot be deduced by another notion, going to a place where there are no parameters, no barriers, and where there are unlimited possibilities.

***

"Thank you for taking the time this evening to hear my ideas. Tonight I'd like to start by talking a little about five basic elements, fire, earth, metal, wood, and water. These are typical and necessary for human life as we know it. I'll also talk about interaction, movement, change and development, stability, predictability, and control of these elements."

"Next, how to destroy and overcome tradition beliefs behind these theories, and creating an imbalance to break down the historical nature that's embedded in the human psyche. If this can be done then we can go beyond the normal to explore spaces and places never understood by anyone before we understand what we've found. So, if we're ready I'll begin with a short visual presentation to wet your appetite, after which I'll begin my talk, then answer your questions."

"Okay, first, let's talk about arguments, reasoning, and deduction. We all grow up learning from others, and there are two sides to this. One is sped up to a point to where we can compress all the information that is known to humankind. Two, it's limited because there's information that hasn't been discovered, so the only way to find this information and knowledge is to begin from nothing. I like to compare this strategy to music. For example there are very few notes, but arrangement of them has unlimited changes. Or, how in chess there are a limited number of pieces, and movement of them is structured, so the end result depends on placement of the moves."

As Michael listened to Professor Paris he felt a connection, and every fiber in his body came alive. It was similar to the classes he'd taken, and looked as if he were going in and out of consciousness while still listening clearly to the professor. Michael felt he knew what the audience wanted to ask before the professor said it, and could read them to the point of even what they were thinking.

"So, I now invite all of you to go on a treasure hunt with me," Professor Paris said, "a treasure hunt for unlimited knowledge and potential to find the secrets that are hidden deep in our mind. Control is how we steer, no matter if by car, boat, just walking through a park. We decide and make choices that impact everything however small or large, important or mundane. Take to heart that we have control, we decide, and if we let others do the deciding for us we lose the power to go where we really want because the decisiveness is muddied if we relinquish, give in, or up."

Michael leaned over toward Sue. "This guy is amazing," Michael whispered."I remember his classes from school."

"He sure has some different ideas," Sue said. "I thought you'd like him because of what you've been telling me about these things."

"How do you feel about him, and what he talked about?"

"He's okay, I guess," Sue said. "What he spoke about seems to make sense."
"I feel like I know him, like we've met in another life or something," Michael said. "I had the same feelings when I met, and had classes with him at school."

The professor continued. "Let's look at how to put a systematic approach to this. It seems that learning follows the same order increases when problems need to be solved, activated when existing knowledge is used as a springboard for new discoveries, and when functions can be demonstrated, promoted, and applied to basic and variable methods."

Michael listened to Professor Paris having a trance like experience. Almost like knowing what he was saying before he said it. Michael's lips moved, shadowed the professor's words silently as they escaped his mouth.

"A practice is a specific function and a program includes some of these actions. One way to see how this works is mind mapping. We can make connections using this system, and knowing that it worked in the past it should be a reliable way to know the end result. All men are mortal; Socrates is a man; Socrates is mortal. Laws and rules are either followed because of consequence, they have design purpose, but if ignored can be devastating or the ideal reality."

Sue nudged Michael with her elbow. "Michael, stop it," she said. "People are starting to watch us."

He was shaken like a wind storm had stopped time, his hand went to his brow, and wiped the beads of sweat that were forming. "Man, that was something else," he whispered, ending with a shiver, and folded his arms in front.

"I think we should go, Michael," Sue said.

"No, I want to stay, and see if I can meet him, and talk. Let's stay a little longer."

"Okay, but if you start acting weird again, we're leaving."

"Don't worry, I'm fine now," Michael said. "Let's listen."

"Heuristics sometimes fail and we need to find another way to solve problems. Rational thinking fails because things are always changing, and old systems cannot keep up with theories that eventually crash. Two important factors for positive results are speed and efficiency. Of course energy is the driving force to make things happen.

Our minds are hardwired and lean toward caution, we want to be safe. If I think the world is centered around us, this shapes thought patterns which affect decisions. Survival and reproduction drive existence, confidence and knowledge that we or I myself can travel to other dimensions through our mind."

***

With the presentation over, Professor Paris received a standing ovation, and a crowd lined up to meet and talk to him. Michael stood in line among the audience waiting for his turn. When it happened Michael was greeted with a smile and handshake.

"Hello, Professor Paris," Michael said. "It's nice to see you again, I was your student a while ago, and still really enjoyed listening to you speak tonight, very interesting ideas."

"Well, thank you," Professor Paris said. "Glad you liked it."

"For some reason I get the feeling we've met before," Michael said.

"Yes, we have," Professor Paris said, " maybe in another life and time perhaps."

"No, really, I think we've met, and actually more than once. I've getting a strong connection that I know you."

They looked at each other, a moment. "Would you like me to sign that for you?" Professor Paris, and pointed to the book Michael held in his hand. "I remember you being in my class.

"Oh, sure, thanks," Michael said, and handed the book to Professor Paris. "When is your next talk?"

"You can access my website, and the schedule's in brochure, you can check those places for up coming dates there. Hope you can make it to another event. Have a good evening."

"I'll definitely try to catch another one if it's not too far away."

Sue walked up to Michael, and tapped him on the shoulder. "Hey stranger," she said.

"How was it talking to him? Are you satisfied?"

"After talking with him he said he remembered me. I've never felt this way after meeting anyone else."

"What did he say?"

"Just being nice, and signed his book for me. He's on a speaking tour now, and I like to listen to him again."

"I'm not sure I want to see him again, but you can," Sue said. "Let's get something to eat, and go home."

IDEA OF THE UNIVERSE

Because of the miniscule amount of knowledge humans have absorbed and collected, there is still only a slight idea of what the universe consists of dynamically. All one really has to do is just look around to see there are many unexplained events, endless unknown links that are continuously being searched for and with only limited results.

All of basic history has been studied and researched for as long as humans have existed, and some have more familiarity and insight with a universe concept. For these few able to use knowledge from then to now all while looking up at the sky with wonder of what's out beyond the stars a certain sum of imagination comes into play.

There are basically two areas holding polarizing views, first being religion with faith, second, science backed by experimentation and fact, and they compete for control even today. The quote by Galileo who said, 'Science teaches how the heaven's go, and religion teaches how to to heaven' seems to make a lot of sense.

But all players have a huge stake and have put forth beliefs, or created theory by adding supporting opinions to one side of the argument. We being mere individuals support one of these groups by making our decisions on how strong or weak these opposing positions along with new discoveries that are made.

All knowledge studied and known up to a current time of one's existence is told to us from elders after taking our first breathes, then through parents, teachers, and finally built on information from all of the contacts made in our life. We remember, organize, and argue these ideas, but how do we know what's really true?

At one time many thought the world was flat, and if we sailed too far we'd go off the edge of the earth into an unknown world filled with demons and monsters waiting to kill us. This is what people believed up to a time, and how everyone was controlled by the leader or lord of the land.

As with the hereafter and what happens to us when and after we die no one's returned to tell anyone, or what to expect when that ultimate experience happens. A lot of beliefs about that irrevocable time mostly come from imagination because returning from the dead has not come about as of yet.

Any stories of returning from the hereafter come from writings, books from the past, and a few wild stories. We know a good imagination can come up with some pretty amazing things, and it's possible to make others believe a good legend or myth.

So throughout life we have some questions to ponder; a place where we can begin is imagination. Questions like what are humans, where did we come from, how do we relate to the universe? What's the real purpose of all we know, and have learned over time? Is there a purpose? Is time random? Can it be changed?

Actually we really don't know that much about any of this if we consider the size and vastness of what's out there beyond the beyond. We're really, nothing, and everything, just like grains of sand or drops of water compared to what we don't understand, and dimensions to some degree seem to be limited to three maybe four. But are there more?

Talk of string theory and vibrations that separate all of the dimensions is an interesting new concept a bit difficult to grasp at first, and has been compare to radio frequencies. For example, like air all around us are signals that float in space, but we can't see any them because we're connected to a different unknown frequency.

So, is this universe group of strings that vibrate is it only a place we occupy one at a time, and is it possible to jump from one string to another? Why haven't we figured this out yet? Will we ever? Maybe there are a few who control what's happening, and it's kept secret from average humans.

All of our senses react to the environment, and certain unique feelings touch us when a connection is made through our senses and emotions. We can control these moments to a degree, and at times it's spontaneous, only happening just at that moment.

We completely open our minds to these basic examples of contact from a human capability perspective. We've learned and studied this, day after day, time after time, but the jury is left wondering on what verdict to choose.

Knowledge dribbles out leaving us asking the same old questions. Can we go beyond what seems limited by human existence? Just asking these questions show we know something more than we think we know. But, well, some things are only fulfilled in dreams like the one you are having now.

***

Michael walked in the direction of a tall wooden door, and next to door stood a barefoot man wearing a long white robe. Around his neck a gold chain, and hanging from it an amulet he held in his hand while carrying a wide smile. "Hello," the man said, in a voice Michael recognized, and had heard before in other dreams he'd had.

"Hi," Michael said, adding, "Where am I? Where is this place?"

"You created this place," he said, "while you were asleep. And this is the beginning of your journey, but to continue on you must pass through a door."

"Where does the door lead," Michael asked.

"I only open the door," the man said. "Where it leads is up to you. You decide, and make that choice yourself."

"Does it go to a good place, bad place, happy place, sad place, dangerous place? Can I know any information ahead of time?"

"I can only say it's all up to you," he said. "Things change randomly and suddenly here. A moment can last an infinite time, or be finished at the blink of an eye because this is a dream you've created. It's all up to your imagination, and how well you can control it is your choice."

"So, I open a door, and just walk through?"

"No, I'll do that for you," he said. "You can't open any doors now, not as yet, but as your ability in this place improves you will open doors, actually, soon, many doors to many places. Just for now you only walk through the door that I open."

"Don't I need to know how to solve a riddle or something? Isn't that how it usually works?"

"No, that's not necessarily true," he said. "No riddles to solve here. Just ask me to open the door and walk through."

"Can I change my mind if I don't like it where it goes? Can I come back here?"

"This is where the journey begins, not where it ends. There will be a different door opening a way to leave.

And you may never see this place again because that's up to you as well."

"Guess I'll go then," I said. "Okay, open the door."

"Very good," the man said. "Enjoy your journey."

Through the door and rising smoke that blurred his vision Michael turned for one last look at the door he'd just gone through because he wanted to ask about an exit. In that moment he found himself alone, standing at the edge off a forest, and in the distance saw some buildings.

Do I go that way toward the building, or back through the woods?

He contemplated on what to do as a wagon pulled by six horses galloped up and stopped. He stood waving away the cloud of dust that had caught up with the coach as it engulfed the coach, driver, and himself.

"Need a ride?" the driver asked.

"Not sure," Michael said. "Where are you heading? You going to that town I in the distance? Is that a town? What's the name of it?"
"Lot's of questions," the driver said. "It is a town, and yes we're going there."

"Oh yeah, one more question. What's the name of it?"

"That's Dodge City."

"Well, I should've guessed, Michael said. "It all seems

to fit because that's what I was thinking even before you said the name."

"I don't know what you're talking about," the driver said, "but hop in if you like, and hold on."

Michael opened the coach door to see a man dressed in black sitting on the right, and a girl dressed in an eloquent manner sitting on the left.

"Hello," he said, and they returned the greeting, both of them moving to accommodate me. Michael looked them over thinking where he should sit, and decided to choose the space next to the girl.

"You ready down there," the driver's voice boomed.

Michael grabbed the door, slammed it shut, and yelled, "All clear down here." With that the driver screamed at the horses, and they bolted, throwing all of in the coach around in different directions.

After we found smoother ground, Michael introduced himself. "Hello, I'm Michael Colt."

"That's interesting," the man in the black suit said. "Are you related to the gun maker?"

Michael smiled and said, "I was always told that by my grandfather, but not sure if he was just telling me story to make it interesting. So, short answer is I don't know."

"You'd be pretty wealthy if you were," the girl said.

"That's for certain," the man in the black suit said.

"I'm Susan Kick," the girl said. "My father has a saloon in Dodge.

"Well," Michael said. "I'll probably be seeing you there at some point then, being that I like drinking."

"What about you," Michael said to the man in the black suit? "Who do I have the pleasure of speaking to?"

The man in the black suit was silent, only staring at Michael Colt, then said, "Voritch," in a German accent. "Call me, Voritch."

"Nice to meet you," and extended his hand in a casual way.
Voritch took Michael's hand and shook it with no words spoken, then released the grip.

"So, Ms. Kick you live in Dodge? You grew up there?"

"Yes, that's right," she said. "What about you?"

"I'm from a small town called Hungry Point."

Voritch's ears perked up, he looked at Michael. "I've been there many times, but not for some while. How are things there? Are you coming from Hungry Point?"

"Things don't change much in Hungry Point," Michael said. "I guess when you live in a place for a long time things don't seem to change because it happens gradually. Don't seem to notice change when it does happen."

"I love change," Voritch said. "Without it you're dead. I need something new not old."

"Fair enough, I agree to a point," Michael said, "but memories are something we can cherish for our lifetime. They never leave even after we're gone because they're carried onward into the future by people we've met, had relationships with, and been influenced by."

"Yes, in a way memories are important, but sometimes they should be wiped clean," Voritch said. "What's your opinion Miss?"

"I have good and bad memories," Sue said. "Memories I've learned from, and some I'd like to forget, but they're part of me, and made me who I am."

"Well said young lady," Voritch said. "Memories are the lifeline to the past."

The coach pulled into Dodge, and stopped in front of the saloon that the girl ran with her father J. Kick.

"Alright everyone," the driver said. "This is the last stop, grab your things, and you, Mister, have to pay for the ride. Go into office there and give this to them. It says the amount you have to pay."

Michael took the paper from the driver. "Sure, I'll go there now, and pay."

"I'd like to see you again, Susan," Michael said.

"Call me Sue."

***

Michael walked in the direction of a tall wooden door. Next to the door is a barefoot man wearing a long white robe. Around his neck a gold chain, and hanging from it, an amulet he held in his hand while displaying a wide smile.

"Hello," the man said, in a voice Michael recognized, and had heard time and time again in other dreams.

I'm sure I've seen him before; in fact I know I have.

"Welcome back, Michael."

"Thanks," Michael said. "Have I been here before?"

"The man in the robe laughed. "You come here all of time. Are you ready for another journey?"

"I guess that's why I'm here," he said.

"The man opened the door, and Michael walked through as he'd done before. Looking back to see the door gone, vanished completely, and no way back as he waited for what ever was to come next. A coach with horses pulled up and stopped, but this one was different from the other times. It was from an earlier time and trimmed with silver. The driver wore a black cloak, cape and hat, his face barely visible. In the distance there was castle on a high point floating in the clouds and mist.

"Evening Sir," the driver said.

"Are you going to that castle," Michael asked.

"Yes," the driver said. "Would you be looking for a ride?"

"I would," Michael said, and got into the coach.

And like before there was a man dressed in black, wearing a dark gray hat, white shirt and tie. A girl elegantly decorated in an elaborate gown with lace and large hat that sometimes concealed her face when she wanted.

"Hello," Michael said, and climbed into the coach.

"The girl nodded. "Hello," she said, then smiled slightly.

Michael turned toward the man and greeted him. "Hello."

He shook his head in disgust, then laughed. "Did I say do something funny?" Michael asked.

The man looked at Michael. "You're here, that is what's funny. Let's get on with it," he said, and took the cane he held rapping the ceiling of the coach to signal the driver we were ready to go. "Let'd move!"

"Have either of you been to this place before?" Michael asked.

"We've all been to this place before," the man in black said, and showed his annoyance again. "We keep doing this, over and over, again and again."

"You do look familiar, but I'm not sure we've met," Michael said.

"Is there something you don't like about me? You seem agrivated."

"Everything, everything about you," the man in black said. "I'm afraid it's you that stands in my way. Without you, I would be able to do anything, but you keep showing up, time after time."

"Don't mind him," the girl said. "My name is Susan, and it's nice to meet you."

"Why do you do this over and over?" the man in black said. "What's the point?"

"You can only talk here, and have no power," Susan said. "So, as I was saying, 'it's nice to meet you,'"

"Call me, Michael."

"Nice to meet you, Michael," Susan said to more groans from the man in black.

"What a waste of time," the man in black said.

Susan was annoyed by the man's nonchalant attitude.

"What's your name, sir?"

The man in black leaned forward toward Michael.

"Voritch," he said.

"Does that name ring a bell for you?"

"I do know you," Michael said, then a surge went through him creating a shiver in the coach, and he clenched his fists.

"Oh," said the man in black watching Michael. "In a fighting mood, are we?"

"Shut up Voritch," Michael said. "I know what you want."

The coach hit the cobble stone narrow village streets twisting and turning like a ride in a theme park. It clanked and clanged, shoving Michael into Susan, they smiled and laughed, then the coach stopped hitting its mark like after the crack of a whip.

"We're here folks," the driver said, all stepped out of the coach, and stood looking up at the castle's stone bulwark that rose before them.

"Have an enjoyable evening," the driver said, and rolled down the hill, and disappeared in the mist.

"Now what," Michael said.

"We go in," Voritch said, "and do the same tap dance all over again."

They walked into the huge entrance of the castle. Hanging from the ceiling above was an iron candelabra with candles, flames glowing, and waving from a breeze coming through the open door. And under it a long wooden table, and at the end a gigantic stone fireplace giving the impression of an endless straight highway leading to the mountains.

Michael was intrigued by the stone fireplace examining the way it was built, and he recognized the style. His grandfather, Poppi, could have built it.

Michael walked closer to get a better look at the fireplace as Susan and Voritch followed on either side of the table. The sound of a door opening and footsteps coming down the staircase echoed through the room, then from a door on the opposite of the room a man entered.

***

Again Michael walked in the direction of a tall wooden door. Standing next to door was a barefoot man wearing a long white robe. Around his neck a gold chain, and hanging from it an amulet he held in his hand while carrying a wide smile. "Hello," the man said, in a voice Michael recognized, and had heard before in other dreams.

"Would you like to go through a door," the man in the robe asked.

"Just one door?" Michael asked. "Can't go through more than one?"

"One at a time," the man in the robe said. "Remember?"

"Okay," Michael said. "Why not?" and walked through the door into clouds and mist, and as before the doors all vanished when he turned back.

As the view became clear he realized that he was in front of a church, and looked up when the bell in the tower rang. The church was cathedral in that the outside was made of stone, and had huge stain glass window placed above the three main wooden doors. It was an enormous old looking structure.

I wonder what's happening inside. Michael thought, and walked up the steps, opened the door to the sound of an organ playing what sounded like wedding music all while the bells in the tower rang. He looked at his arms, then down at his feet, and discovered he wore a tuxedo.

What's this? he thought. *Who's getting married?*

He was greeted by a woman who seemed frantic and relieved. "We've been waiting for you," she said.

"What took you so long to get here?"

"Sorry, I lost track of time," Michael said.

"Well," she said. "You've got to go through that door," she pointed.

Then down the stairs, walk to the front, up the stairs, and into your position."

"Get into position for what?"

She smiled, and said, "No time for joking around. You know why you're here. Just go please, and get into positon."

Michael pointed to confirm where to go. "I go through that door?"

"Yes, yes, yes," she said. "Hurry, hurry, go, go," and gestured with her arm.

Michael followed her instructions. *What is this all about? I just don't understand.*

After climbing the stairs he opened the door to a packed church filled with relatives, friends, some famous people, actors, and writers he'd admired.

This is a wedding, he thought, and closed the door. *Is it my wedding*?

The organ began to play the march, he opened the door to see a woman in a long flowing wedding gown and veil covered face, slowly walked down the aisle.

Who is that?

From behind a voice said, "It's time to go."

Michael turned and saw a priest and altar boys standing behind ready to march out to the front of the church. On the other side of the rectory was Moses giving the thumbs up while showed the ring then put it back in his pocket.

They all marched out together, and down to the front watching the bride make her way. Moses smiled at

Michael, nodding in agreement that this was the thing to do. The bride stopped and Michael joined her, and after the priest made a few comments, Michael lifted the veil.

***

Once again Michael walked in the direction of a tall wooden door. Next to the door is a barefoot man wearing a long white robe. Around his neck a gold chain, and hanging from it an amulet he holds in his hand while carrying a wide smile.

"Hello," the man said, in a voice Michael recognized, and had heard before in other dreams. Then he sat up in bed struggling to remember what he'd dreamed about. He stood and walked to the window, feeling a cool breeze wrap around his body, then looked at the bed where sue was sleeping soundly.

What will I dream next, he thought.

***

He looked up and found that he was at the airport.

What am I doing here?

It was busy, and Christmas decorations were hanging all around, lights blinking, and people laughing, enjoying life, excited about traveling. As Michael walked through the airport wondered which city he was in.

Then he saw schedule board monitors listing all of the flights, and made his way in that direction. I'm back here again. Is there's no way out?

THE COMPOUND

Mixtures, formulas, and compounds make up all of the parts that create the scene from the ceiling to the floor, where he noticed the brass spittoons in strategic locations where they waited as targets of tobacco spatter.

There was enough space to accommodate a fairly large number of people in the saloon, and usually it had a good crowd. Just like most places like this there was a huge mirror covering the wall behind the bar, and in front of it, bottles of just about any kind of booze one could imagine lined up like soldiers used to on the battlefield.

Michael turned jolted by the voice of the bartender.

"What'll you have?" Who asked while standing there seemingly in a hurry to move on and serve other customers.

"A beer," Michael said, and watched the glass filled to the brim, spill, and be topped off. The bartender placed the glass in front of Michael.

"Need anything else?"

"No, this is fine, thanks. Not too crowded in here."

"It's still early," the bartender said as he moved on filling another glass.

"Early," Michael said with some disbelief. "How late are you open?"

"Here you go," the bartender said, sliding another glass down the bar.

"Were open until everyone leaves, and that's two-bits for the beer."

Michael put a coin on the bar, raised his glass to toast, and took a drink of the precious ale, sipping the foam from the glass careful not to spill any.

He watched the bartender do the bar-room ballet, serving customers from behind the bar to the music of the crowd noise, then turned to see what was happening behind.

Observing more people filling the place now, and a guy with a handlebar moustache, a gold vest and derby, playing the piano on the other side of the room. Michael made his way to the table where Voritch was sitting.

"Mind if I join you?"

Voritch gesture to the chair across from him said, "Be my guest. We can always use some new blood, " he laughed, "and new money in the game." He gave a look of being ready to fleece the other players.

Michael slid the chair back and dropped into view across the table from Voritch. "Thanks,
"You plan on being in town for a while?" Voritch asked.

Michael looked up. "I don't have any fixed plans," Michael said. "Just trying to win a little cash, how about you?"

"I have some business to attend to, then moving on."

"What kind business are you in?"

"The transportation business; it's a family business, and we deal with all modes of transportation. At the moment we're building our railroad business."

"What do you do for the railroad?"

"Mainly look for places to extend the line? We think this town has potential to be a hub. They're running a lot of cattle through here. I convince farmers and landowners to sell their property to us."

"Not sure how that's done, but you're probably right, and if that's the situation you have a way to move the cattle east." Michael said, and took a drink of his beer.

"You know I get the feeling that we've met before today. You get that feeling at all?"

"I don't know," Voritch said. "What makes you think that?" What kind of feelings are you having?"

"I don't know, just a gut feeling I've got, and I'm usually right about things like that."

Voritch looked at Michael. "Look around. You know where you are, don't you? What does your gut feeling say about that?"

"I'm in Dodge," Michael said. "It's an important town for the people who live here, and for business."

"Right, you're in Dodge. Have you been here before?"

"Why do I get the feeling you know something I don't? Am I wrong or right," Michael said, and looked around the saloon.

"How did you get here?" Voritch asked.

"On the same stagecoach as you," Michael said.

"I was on the stagecoach before you," Voritch said.

"Where were you before getting on? Can you remember? Coming back to you at all?"

Michael thought back and remembered the door, the man in the white robe, and the chain with the amulet that was around the man's neck.

"I just remember walking through a door, then the coach pulling up, and I got on after talking to the driver."

"Good," Voritch said. "Good, you remember. Do you recall who opened the door?"

"For some reason I remember a man in a white robe?"

"Who is the man in the robe, and what did he say to you?"

"I don't know, and can't recall what he talked about. I guess nothing really relevant as far as I remember."

"Well," Voritch said, "let me fill in some gaps, and close some of the holes for you."

"Yeah, why don't you do that for me?" Michael straightened and sat back, his demeanor change to a defensive reaction. "Fill in the gaps for me."

"Have you heard of the professor? If not, I guarantee he knows us, and has the item that controls this world that we're in now."

"What do you mean by this world we're in?"

"You really have no idea who you are or where you come from, or what you're doing here? You understand that what happening now is all from a dream," Voritch said, and raised his arms in a slow movement through the air, gesturing to everything around the room.

"You still have no clue what is happening, do you?"

"A dream? What do you mean this is a dream?"

"I know it seems so real to us, but that's how dreams work. Dreams are a journey, searching for something that can control this world and maybe in this dream you're looking for me." Voritch said, and took drink.

"Actually, I believe you've been looking for me for a long time, but that'll change in the future. Soon it'll be me looking for you."

"Why would you be looking for me?"

"To get what belongs to me. I've had it, lost it, and I want it back. It's mine, and I want it! No amount of assistance from you or the professor will help because in the end it'll be me who controls this place not him or you. And, after I have control here can operate in the physical world as well."

"You've lost me," Michael said.

"That's easy to do," Voritch said. "Will meet another time, and the original amulet will be mine for the taking." Voritch stood, drank the last of the whisky in his glass, and walked out of the saloon.

He turned once more before going through the saloon

door, and said,

"You are weak, Michael Colt, you want comfort, and you never stand your ground. You will always be weak, and this will be a sweet victory for me."

Michael was left confused and puzzled on what had just happened when the girl he'd met on coach came into the saloon. She smiled when her eye caught Michael, then she walked to his table.

"Nice seeing you again," Michael said. "Want to sit and talk a while?"

"Sure, so, how's your first day in Dodge?"

"I've been here before, memories are coming back, and just had the strangest conversation with Voritch."

"Why, what did he say?"

"I can't even repeat it because it was so strange, but I know I've seen him before, and met you before too, haven't I?"

"I think it's time," she said.

"Time for what?" Michael asked.

"To wake up," she said, before giving him a firm slap across the face, then his eyes opened, he sat up in bed, and looked as if he'd returned from another world.

"What the hell just happened?

PEACE & TRANQUILITY

After thinking about what he'd heard, and remembering from the dreams he'd been having, Michael had a strong desire to understand things more clearly. *I just know there's more to all of this*, he thought as he drove.

In most of his dreams he recalled the silhouettes of figures clad in curious mystic white robes who wore gold chains with shimmering amulets around their necks, and when they spoke, an unknown exotic language fell from their lips.

Also, from memory, these people in his dreams seem to resemble what he thought to be images of wizards, and more than just mere men. And one he remembered by name was Voritch, and it echoed in the dreams he'd had, and all of this was burned into his brain, but wasn't sure why.

Michael pondered what was happening. *What does all of this mean? What role does Voritch play in all of this? Who is Voritch?*

In the pieces and clips of dreams he did recall, Vortich wanted something, but whatever he was searching for remained a mystery to Michael. Was Vortich a real person or just an imaginary character he made up in his dreams?

If he is a real person where did I first meet him?

He couldn't put together who the beings were, or where they were from, and nothing meant anything to him. Michael looked up into the midnight sky watching the stars blinking back at him.

"I have to know what this is all about, and what's going to happen next."

Michael stopped, parked, got out and waited a moment as he closed the door to his truck, then made his way to the cabin, focusing on and watching the lights he saw flickering in the windows. *Sue must be here, and still up*, he thought.

Hearing the faint sound of music that carried on the evening air, he climbed the steps to the porch following the beat, his head moving in time. He reached out to test the door, it was unlocked, and he pushed it open to see a dimly lit entrance. "Sue? Are you here?"

"I'm in the kitchen," she said, then asked, "Are you hungry?"

"Yeah, a little," Michael said. "Whatever you're making smells good. Will it be ready pretty soon? I've got a pretty good appetite."

"It's ready now, come on have a seat," she said.

"You're back kind of late. I thought you'd be here earlier. What took you so long?"

"I stopped down by the river to watch the stars," he said. "It makes me feel relaxed, and wonder what's out there. It's especially clear tonight, so the stars are more than visible. I was able to make out shapes of the constellations, well not all of them, but the one's I remember from doing the same thing with Poppi."

"I went out to toss some vegetable scraps out over the fence and thought the same, so I know what you mean, extremely bright tonight." Sue said.

"That's one reason I like coming to the cabin."

"Do ever think about how we met, and how we grew up together," he asked. "What our life means? The odds of us meeting are so minuscule when you think about the size of the universe. Almost a wonder how anyone's life can actually be planned, but if you believe in destiny I guess anything can happen. All kinds of things are happing to people all of the time."

"You're getting pretty deep, Michael. What's wrong? Are you still having the weird dreams?"

"I am and feel like I'm in another world when I dream," he said.

"When I dream I go to a world that seems so real. Tonight while I was looking at the stars I was thinking and dreaming about being in a western town. And real enough to feel like it was happening while I was awake, but also knew I was dreaming, and it was happening in real time at the same time."

"I think that's just a complicated way of just saying daydreaming," Sue said.

"Is it called daydreaming if it happens at night?"

"Funny, funny, ha-ha, how did you feel when that happened? Did you feel you were you experiencing a dream?"

"It felt great," he said. "I was at peace with myself, but part me felt of this world, and part of some kind of dream world."

Sue put two plates on the table and dished up. "Part of this world and part of the dream world, that's a funny way to put it, isn't that the way it is for everyone? Let's eat a little. Food will calm us down and help us relax, and get into our primal mode."

"How are you feeling?" he asked. "I mean it's almost time for the little guy you're carrying to start living in this world. Come to think of it I felt a little like that tonight. Thinking about the world from inside the womb and ready to come out, but do babies think of the world before being born? I don't think a baby can remember that. I have heard of babies listening to classical music, how it's soothing, and encourages a child's learning ability."

"Wow!" she said. "What you're talking about sounds life changing. You had a life changing experience tonight. When something we can't explain happens it's because your life has changed. And being connected to the stars in a sense makes it more universal."

"We always think of being at the beginning of something else," he said.

"Yes, and something much bigger than just a human experience, and a way for us to learn about ourselves, and how we fit in the world as we know it."

"Life is always teaching us about the world."

"Remember I told you about the guy I see, and hear in my dreams?"

"Maybe, I think I remember you saying something or mentioning it."
"Well, it's always the same guy, and I know his name because like I said, I hear it."

"What's the name?" Sue's voice echoed. "What's the name?"

"The name is . . . I can't remember," he said, and fell backward on the bed, his head hitting the pillow softly.

In his dreams, Michael felt safe even though after he

woke, there were always some unusual outcomes.

He closed his eyes and thought, *Where is the one place I'd like to go more than any other? The one place more than any other, more that any other, other.* After a moment his eyes looked into the futur, and he fell into deep sleep.

***

Michael walked in the direction of a tall wide wooden door. Next to the door is a barefoot man wearing a long white robe. Around his neck is a gold chain, and hanging from it an amulet he held in his hand while carrying a wide smile. "Hello," the man said in a voice Michael recognized, and had heard before in other dreams.

After a moment he was in a sunny park with a garden filled with flowers, abundant vegetables for the taking, fruit everywhere, and more strawberries than anyone could ever eat.

Is this the Garden of Eden? he thought. *Looks and feels like it.*

He followed a path along the shore of a pond where every so often a fish would splash, and break through the glassy watery surface. This peaceful quiet place where solitude came easy, in this place no other people could see what was made for him and only him.
It's almost like it was made by me, he thought.

Rabbits and squirrels ran about, birds sang and flew,

and as he looked up ducks above were flying in formation. Michael sat down on the soft grass, then watched water ripple and flow from falling raindrops.

He looked up to sky examining the blanket of clouds. As his face became covered in a steady flow of rain, he looked for shelter, found it next to a stone wall with an overhang, and made his way there out of the rain.

Standing under the stone structure he studied the vine attached to the wall, and noticed a figure moving in the distance. This figure caught his attention as he watched it grow in size; it continued to come closer, and obviously now he could tell it was human, not sure of male or female, but human nonetheless.

As the figure got closer, it now moved with an elegant gate, floating like a dancer on air, then finally in clear view could tell it was a woman. She approached Michael, a look of joy overwhelmed her, then while grabbing and holding on tightly she rubbed her face on his, kissing him fiercely.

At first Michael was stunned, but acquiesced enjoying this time, complying with what had happened, and submitting. With a feeling of flying he continued to let her kiss, and touch him as the rain fell all round.

They broke apart, and stood staring, eyes locked by an invisible link to each other. "Wow," Michael said. "Who are you?"

"She smiled. "I've been waiting the longest time for you," she said.

"Waiting for me," he said. "Why wait for me? Who are you?"

"We've met before," she said. "You don't remember?"

"I don't think we've met because I'd absolutely, undoubtedly, without any question, remember you."

"I look different, but inside I'm the same as I've always been."

"I can't remember, and just don't know who are you?"

"Give me your hand," she said, turned it over, and placed hers on top. Do you feel it?"

"It's warm," he said, and when she pulled her hand away there was a glowing orb shape on both of their hands.

"What is this?' Michael said, and he stepped back. "What did you do? What is this?"

"Nothing that you haven't seen before," she said.

"We've done many things together, and since we found each other have been inseparable."

"Inseparable? Why don't I have any memory of you?"

"You soon will," she said. "You soon will."

"Who are you?" he asked again.

She put the palms of her hands on either side of

Michael's face.

"Close your eyes, and trust me. I will help you remember," then he woke, sat up, and tried to remember the dream he'd just had.

CONVERSATIONS

Occasionally after waking up, voices from dreams that Michael didn't recognize would continue to echo in his ear throughout the day. He felt these voices were familiar, but couldn't connect any of them to a face or to anyone that he knew, so more or less they were the voices of strangers, and unknown shadow entities.

At times he gradually recalled faint outlines of these shadowy figures from his dreams, but after a time even the foggy images along with the unknown voices would fade. As he tried to bring them in focus at the end of the day, a brief left-over disconnected memory remained to haunt him. The images would pop up occasionally at odd times without warning leaving him mystified and lost.

He also dreamed on experiences recalled from the past, and things that happened while growing up in Hungry Point. Dreams of times with Poppi and Moses out on the river fishing, going on hunting excursions, walking in the woods, or on occasion an evening that was spent at Kick's bar would rise to the top of his memories. These dreams all came from real experiences, but the shadows of figures he remembered had a disconnected feel, or didn't belong to anything. Dreams about Kick's, bar included images of the mounted deer heads racks, stuffed fish on the walls, along with miscellaneous trophies and plaques from softball and pool tournaments. Some had sayings, and inscribed on one plaque above the door was —**You're only a stranger once** —

The dream events began to happen more and more, night after night, again and again. Old memories, special events, and other random things peppered with mixed limited recollections, and unknown events seemed totally oblivious at times, but hinted that he knew where they had originated. They came from somewhere, there was no doubt of that, and there was a reason for being here now.

Occasionally he'd wake up in bed thinking he was in an unknown place, or at times a familiar one somewhere in and around Hungry Point, but he was still in bed when this happened. At times waking up was even a dream, and once he realized this would tell himself to wake up, and finally he'd really be awake.

The more he'd re-wake after sleeping the stranger things felt, and more normal in the dream world. His legs and arms would feel numb similar to phantom limbs without sensory connections as if they belonged to another person. After stretching his muscles to let the blood flow through his body, it seem to act like a machine, turning on and off by obeying commands of thought. He'd go to the kitchen and make something to eat, but actually he was asleep, then wake up in bed as it all turned out to be a dream. It was becoming a time of not knowing reverie from certainty.

There was the occasional dream from atop a high-rise in some random city. He opened his eyes seeing the view of a red Ferris wheel across the way decorating a blue sky as it turned slowly. Stepping closer he saw the street below with people and cars moving and scurrying about.

Judging from the size of those people I see down on the street, I'd say I'm about twenty stories or so high, he thought. *Where am I? What city is this? Where am I?*

A noisy caravan of motorcycles roared by, and a loud speaker preaching something in an unknown language echoed on waves throughout the city.

What country is this? Why is there a Ferris wheel on top of that building? He could see people in the carriages rollong slowly clockwise. *Why am I in this building? Where's the elevator.*

He walked down the maze-like hallway, and thought, *Should I asked for directions.* He began to sweat; feeling lost with no idea of where he was or supposed to go.

"Excuse me, could you tell me where the elevator is?"

"Go straight to the end of the hallway, and turn right, there are three elevators."

"Thanks," he said, then after making his way down the hall he stopped in front of three doors. He pushed the down button to go to the first floor. *This is like the TV game show with door number one, two and three. Will I get a prize*? he thought, and as he stood and examined the cubical the sound of the electric motor and cables whirled. He had no idea where he would end up, images flashed in his mind, all he knew is that he seemed to be traveling to and from somewhere.

Then as the elevator moved a voice said, "How can I help?"

"He looked up at the ceiling to where the voice came from. I'm not sure what you mean? Who are you? What's going on?"

"I can offer you anything you'd like, or make it a surprise."

"I still don't get what you mean? Do I get three wishes or something?"

"When the door opens," the voice said, "would you like a surprise?"

"I can have anything that I'll see after the door opens?" he said.

"Okay, how about a surprise? And what would it be? A bloody body, snakes, a beautiful or old lady, perhaps transport me to a jungle, forest, or faraway land."

The elevator stopped, he had arrived at his destination, and when the doors opened the hallway was empty, no one and nothing, zilch there to attack or scare him out of his socks. He got back in, pushed the button for the first floor. It started down picking up speed, a moment later just as it stopped, the door started to open and he woke and sat up in bed.

Later that morning while in the shower, he watched the water fall down rolling off his body and down the drain. *It's like watching a river and a waterfall, and my body is a mountain*, he thought, then looked down at the drain watching what looked like hair, or some kind of material, seemingly growing out and up around his legs encasing him like a glove.

Wake up! Wake up, before it covers my head! His voice screamed in his head, an alarm rang, sirens screeched, he woke and turned off the hot tap leaving only cold water spraying in his face. After opening his eyes he woke, sat up in bed with wet hair, watching water dripping from his hands and body. "Was that shower experience a dream too? I'm not sure what is real and what is a dream?" he whispered

There was a repeating voice, just like he'd heard in the elevator and sounded the same as in other dreams, there was some connection to him, but the link to it was missing. Every time just when he thought he'd discover who the voice belonged to, the dreamed stopped, and he woke.

Whose voice is that? he thought. *I know it, so familiar, I think.* He sat on the bed in the dark, unsure as the moonlight crept through the window on a breeze. *Is this a sleeping or waking dream?* he thought, then closed his eyes.

Thunder clapped waking Michael who stared at the window as lightning flashed, then it was quiet when the urge to say, "Hello! Can you hear me?" came over him. Once again he said, "Are you there?" in a tone as if a phone connection had gone static.

"Close your eyes a moment, then open them," a calm low voice said.

"Do I know you," Michael asked.

"Of course you know me," the voice said. "We've met many times in your dreams and in the past."

"Your voice is familiar," Michael said. "I know we've talked, but can't remember about what except for a few pieces of memories nothing sticks. Can you give me more information to help me recall?"

"Soon everything will be clear as long as you continue on this journey," the voice said. We will meet again soon. Remember that you do have some control, and in the future total control."

"You've got to tell me something, at least give me some clues," Michael said, distressed and impatient wanting an answer to this puzzle.

"For the time being I'll just say this, the voice said, "I will take you on a voyage to meet the tribe, and I promise this will be a journey you will never forget."

Michael puzzled asked, "What is the tribe? And journey to where?"

"You will know soon," the voice said. "Now wake up!"

Michael sat up in bed wide eyed staring at the window, the trail of the voice echoed in his head.

"Who was speaking? I think I recognize that voice. Why don't I know who it is?" Michael heard some noise coming from the kitchen. *Must be Sue, home from work*, he thought. "Sue," he said and got out of bed and went into the kitchen.

There she was standing in the kitchen making French Toast. "You just get back?"

"How's everything?" Michael asked. "It's funny how things work out. I was offered a job from your dad, and you were hired instead."

"I remember you not having any interest in the job."

"You're right," Michael said. "It's not area of expertise. Why are you so secret about it? You never talk about what you actually do."

"I can't," Sue said, "because it's secret. That's how secrets work."

"I guess," Michael said. "Is what you're cooking a secret?"

"Yes," Sue said. "Secret French Toast recipe. I'll never tell."

PRISONERS OF SHADOWS

Walking, walking, and more walking along the roadside under glowing street lights that were projecting shifting shadows in a frenzy bouncing all around. *Are they from another world?* Michael watched them come from behind, the side, above, constantly moving as if trying to run away and hide suggesting they were there for some unknown reason or purpose, but without doubt there must be an intention or rationale.

When the question of why shadows exist comes up most will say it's a consequence of light. But I wonder if shadows are they a doorway to another dimension? Pure space as we understand is beyond comprehension of thought for most of us, especially after taking into account its gargantuan vastness.

Michael continued to make his way feeling guided by an outside power while seemingly knowing which direction to go without knowing the destination or reason. He had know idea how this was happening, and questioned himself. *Where am I going, and why?* And other questions popped into his mind, but there were no answers, only more questions.

He looked down at his feet marching along to a beat as if he were with a group of soldiers heading into combat, all along with the added sounds of loud footsteps echoing on the breeze searching for an ear. Every step sounded louder, and seemed to be coming not from one person, but a whole company or brigade, and as he looked around saw no one in sight, there was no one else, only shadows. *Why do I feel this way?*

He stopped, now stood at a crossroads, and a decision had to be made to which direction to attempt or turn, and questioned himself again.

Do I go straight, left, right, back? Can I change my mind after deciding or is this a decision final? He waited listening for his brain to give the command on which way to go, when suddenly he stepped to the left and began to walk. *Why did I choose to go left? Did my feet choose on their own? How do they know how and where to step?*

Up a hill he walked while watching a light glowing dimly in the distance, and it moved away from him as hheaded toward it as if to beckon to follow. Over and over he asks himself, *Am I to follow this light? Is it guiding me somewhere? Where am I going?*

The light moved when he did, and stopped when he stopped. *What is this place?* He looked behind, and below to a road under his feet and nothing, but dark air in the distance with trees appearing on either side with shadows jumping between. And the light ahead still called him, so he continued forward imagining what he'd see before getting arriving wherever he was supposed to be.

He came to another branch in the road and must make another decision to go left or right or back into darkness. Standing there silent waiting for some kind of signal, a sound, or call of any kind giving a clue of what to do. Then he heard a noise from behind, so he turned and listened to the sound of the sea washing to the shore like waves getting louder little by little, louder and louder.

Is that the sign?

This time he chose to go right, and there ahead was the light blinking what looked like a Morse code message.

What does it mean?

Then the light illuminated a tunnel of trees with more shadows dancing, then he heard a stream of water flowing.

Michael felt a hand resting on his shoulder, but he was alone as far as he could tell, then a man's voice said.

"Don't go to the light. If you continue to follow the light you'll never leave this place."

He was hesitant to turn and see who is touching his shoulder, but curiosity won, he pivoted, and standing there smiling like an old friend was the professor.

"What is this place?" Michael asked.

"This is where lost minds travel never to return," the professor said.

"All thoughts and ideas end if you go there, and memories are footprints that lead to a trail for nowhere. Thanatos abides in this place called the prison of the dead."

"So, if I follow the light, and go down the tunnel, I'll never leave?"

"No one ever has, and you'd be the first if it is possible at all. We're all special; maybe you're the chosen one, but I think you know that."

"I don't know that," Michael said. "How would I know what's special."

"I say you should think and look back, remember your past, your father, grandfather, and other things that have happened."

"I don't remember my father because he died when I was very young, but have many pleasant memories with my grandfather, Poppi?"

"You know the truth about your father, your grandfather, and the time before that. It's all in your memory, all in the past, and that will make your future."

"I have dreams, but vaguely remember them."

"They will become clear as time goes by."

"How can I do that? What do I need to do?"

"Just think about what comes to mind, let yourself go, it'll just come out and you'll be free."

"I don't know how to do that?"

"I can help you with a few clues to spark your thoughts."

HELIOCENTRICITY

How do you know the earth revolves around the sun? Probably because it's what we've been told from our youth. First by looking in books, photographs, and movies, then seeing the shapes while they form in the night sky.

People say just look at the sky, and that tells you the sun is at the center of the system we live in. Then we think of where we are in this system. This image boggles the mind because the earth is just a speck in the Milky Way, an open endless space full of everything.

There haven't been any universal travelers to explain in detail what really is out in the vast expanse we see. So if earth is such a minor player, and just a speck, what is going on with us on this planet? Why are there stories of alien landings, old artifacts that are studied, but not understood, and a yearning to know where humans came or evolved from? No one knows, some care, others reflect.

We only have a cursory knowledge of our ancestors and hardly a minuet understanding of who we are because it's all a mystery. So, let's take a trip, a journey, and voyage to another place that's been just as elusive to us as our thoughts which melt away with time.

"Come on." a voice said. "You can make it."

The boy looked over the landscape carefully following the sound of the voice, testing each step as he moved down a slope on a narrow path.

"Come on," the same voice said.

Slowly down a path the kid went sliding and slipping, catching himself before falling when he came to a tree that sat right in the middle of the trail. With one arm balancing on the tree he walked around it, but lost his footing, fell, and rolled down the hill. After stopping flat and on his back, the boy opened his eyes to the blue sky and heard the voice again.

"Are you okay?"

He sat up, stood and brushed off the dirt, then turned back to where he saw a house, looked at the path and the road waiting at the bottom of the hill. *I wonder where that road leads*, the boy thought, and made his way down testing each step on the steep terrain.

At the bottom he encountered a split in the path, and heard voices coming from both directions. Standing there confused and wondering if he should go back from where he came or go left or right on the new path. This was the first time he'd felt like this or been in this situation as far as he knew. Where it was all up to him, where he he made all of the choices.

He waited hoping his feet would decide for him, or that there might be some clue, a signal telling him what to do. And perhaps it made no difference which way he chose, and the outcome would be the same no matter which trail he took.

"This is the path to choose," a familiar voice echoed from the narrow road on the right.

Guess I'll go that way, the boy thought, and as he stepped on the path, the view in front changed into a garden with a small stream flowing by with flowers of all colors, shapes, and sizes surrounding him completely.

The scent in the air had a natural perfume aroma, the sky blue holding puffy clouds as a light breeze waddled through the tall grass.

Where am I? he thought, and looked at his hands which now were larger because he had aged into a young man. He knelt at the stream looking at his face somewhat distorted by the ripples of water. He seemed to change more, getting older and older.

Who or what am I becoming? he thought.

From behind there was the sound of footsteps, and he turned to see a man he recognized. *Professor*, he thought, with a slight uncertainty.

"Hi kid, remember me? Luke, Luke Paris,"

"You look like a guy I used to know called the professor."

"You can call me that if you like," Luke said, "been called much worse."

Michael stood, stared at Luke Paris for a time, then raised his arm, and pointed. "I think the last time we were in this place I sat under that tree over there."

"You remember," Luke said. "Yes, we were under that tree, and what did we talk about?"

"But at that time I was young, just a kid, and you were old. We've changed places. I'm older, and you're younger."

"Seems that way, doesn't it?" Luke said. "What do you think all of this means?"

"I don't know," Michael said. "This is all confusing to me.

Luke walked over and sat in the place under the tree where Michael had been the time they'd met before.

"This is a comfortable spot," he said. "I understand why you chose it last time."

"I'm still confused," Michael said. "I'm starting to remember that time.

It was right after that guy had tried to do something to us, and you stopped him."

"That's right! We stopped him, near this spot, right here."

"Why are you here again? Why am I here? Why are we doing this again?"

"On that day you decided not to learn more, not to know more," Luke said. "You wanted to stay young."

"I didn't want to control the future of the world," Michael said.

"Well the forces that be have sent me back to change your mind," Luke said.

"Changed my mind to do what?"

"That's why we've changed places," Luke said.

"You're going to see for yourself, and hopefully come to think that this is a noble cause to pursue. Only you can do what you need to do."

"You sat under this tree, and went back to the beginning, essentially changing the outcome of what we worked on together."

"Now it's your turn to go back and see why."

"What if I don't?"

"You're aging, and at a fast pace," Luke said. "If you want to continue to live you've got to go and see for yourself. Only they can help you."

"They?" Michael said. "Who?"

"Members of the tribe," Luke said. "There are ten, and one of them who seeks to rule all, must be stopped. You may remember, under the name, Otto."

"How do I get to this place you're talking about?"

"Close your eyes," Luke said. "Say the magic words."

"I don't know the magic words."

"It's the name of their world, their home, only the chosen few get to see it. I promise you won't regret going there."

"I remember now," Michael said. "You floated away on a beam of light, and vanished into space. I stayed here under this tree, then went back to my life as a kid. Seems like just a moment ago."

"You were never a kid," Luke said. "You were chosen like others before you."

"Why can't you be chosen?"

"I'm here to do something else now," Luke said, "but you're here to save Rim Stone."

"Rim Stone?" Michael asked. "What's that? How do I get there?"

"Close your eyes, and you'll be on your way."

"Will I have this life back?"

"You'll always have this life, and all the lives you've lived. You'll recall everything after you meet the tribe. Decide soon because you're aging quickly, not much time left for you here. After a certain point it'll be too late, and you'll never get this chance again."

Michael saw his hands aging, the skin covering his face and hands growing old, and when he removed them stood on a beam of light slowly moving away from Luke.

Luke waved, "You made the right choice, Michael," he said, and threw the line from the fishing pole into the river. "I'll be waiting here for you. You won't regret what you've done, and you'll know everything you need to help the tribe get their world back."

Michael walked toward the river bank, stood there a moment, turned once to see the tree, and Luke Paris under the tree. He raised his had, waved, and stepped into the river.

The water rose around his legs, then to his neck, and finally over his head. A bell echoed in the sky.

DREAM FIGHT

"No! No! No!" Michael yelled after being dragged off the sofa, then his face hit the floor and he woke up.

"What the hell what was that?" he said, then rolled over, sat up, and looked around waiting for his eyes to adapt to darkness. "Who's there?" He felt someone, or something, in the room, but no one seemed to be there, at least no one he could see, just an empty semi-dark room.

"I'm alone," he said, and after scanning the room to make sure of that, he noticed his arm and hand being sore. He stretched, then massaged it from the shoulder down to the wrist. "Must be sore from helping Moses with the job yesterday. I lifted, put down and set quite a bit of stone. It's probably from that. It can't hurt this much from rolling off the sofa."

Then Michael began to recall that in the dream he'd had. Remembering not only falling, but a feeling of being pulled off the sofa by someone or something.

"That sure seemed real to me."

"What time it is?" He looked across the room at the window and only saw a reflection of a starry sky, then glanced at his watch.

"Two o'clock."

More parts of the dream were coming back. Bits and pieces with images of a shadowy figure that he rememembered, and how it let go of his arm as he woke. He rubbed his sore arm again.

"That dream was so real! Like there actually was someone pulling me, and taking me to another place, but where, and who was it?"

Why am I dreaming of this? Don't feel like sleeping now, so might as well get up.

He had been staying at the cabin in Hungry Point helping Moses with a few local jobs. He was thinking about the dream when the phone rang, and that startled him a moment. It rang again, he stood, picked up the receiver, and answered with some hesitation.

"Hello," he said while clearing his throat.

"Michael? Are you okay? What's up?"

"Sue," he said, surprised that she called. "I'm fine,

just woke up. It's pretty early for you to be calling. Everything okay with you?"

"I had the strangest dream," she said.

"Me too," Michael said. "Do you remember what your dream was about?"

"Not really," she said. "All I remember is waking up because it felt like was being dragged somewhere."

"Dragged? That's strange," he said. "I had a dream like that too, and woke up on the floor, but don't recall much else, just the feeling of being dragged off the sofa, then I woke up on the floor after landing on my face. Not something that's happened to me very often, but I think I fell off the sofa."

"A bit strange that we both had similar dreams," she said. "That's never happened, especially on the same night at around the same time. Are you coming back to the apartment today or staying at the cabin?"

"I was planning on staying and helping Moses with a job, but I can leave and head back if you want."

"Don't worry everything is fine. How about I head to the cabin later? Sue said. "You want some company?"

"Great, sure," he said. "I'm meeting Moses in town this morning, and we're getting some grub before going to the job. What time will you be here?"

"Maybe later, sometime in the afternoon. I'll stop by

the grocery store to pick up some food and make lunch. What would you like to have?"

"Anything's fine," he said.

"Okay, I'll make a list of stuff, and head there. See you later."

"Okay, drive carefully, see you later today."

Michael put the phone down, walked to the window, and watched the darkness above slowly changing to soft light blue sky. "Looks like it's shaping up to be a nice day, and I should get a lot done."

As he watched the sunrise, memories from the past flooded through his mind in a steady stream of thought. First was a reflection of falling on the path that led down to the road from a house, and the point halfway where it encircled the tree that stood halfway down the hill to the sidewalk.

I remember standing and falling by that tree, he thought, *but not how old I was*?

From that perspective the house and street could be seen. It was a two-story older structure with another tree in front of it, and windows with a number of divided glass lites on either side of a double wooden French door. A wire fence separated a pasture that had cows grazing in the distance, and a horse stood with its head stretched over the fence while nibbling at the grass. The siding of the house was a kind of shingle-siding and whole design looked European.

Images of a small kid about four or five standing in a kitchen with his shoes untied flashed when he closed his eyes. He was wearing oversized jeans with suspenders, and long sleeve T-Shirt.

Is that me? I think it is.

There was a dog, a German Shepard sitting next to the boy, ready to obey his commands. *What was his name?* Michael tried but couldn't remember. The only thing he did remember was the nasty way the dog had died. He hadn't seen how it happened, but heard from someone, maybe his mother, that the dog had cut its throat after getting its head stuck in a can while trying to eat whatever was left in the can. It was a sad time, but soon a new dog was there, a black and brown mixed collie, who liked sleeping on the porch.

A back porch with a restaurant connected to a bar suddenly emerged, then the image floated away, and now he was playing on a truck tire in front of a garage. Scattered all around were more old tires and rims, some metal others made of wood most likely from farm wagons and equipment.

In the back stood a concrete building, and inside a car with parts missing waiting for repair. A moment later the image disappeared, and he was watching a guy cutting boards trying to fit them into an old car that looked like an old Ford Model -T

Is that my dad?

Now it all changed again and there was a ranch style house, painted brown and yellow, with a garage just to the right. Suddenly a dog ran from the vegetable garden barking chasing after a cat. A guy in a brown car pulled up to the house. He greeted the people who were standing and sitting on the porch.

He wore a dark blue suit, white shirt and tie, and talking about coming from some kind of formal event. Around his neck the man had a camera dangling which he took in hand and snapped the boy's picture.

Who is that? I think he's a relative?

The man talked with the people, and took more pictures, arranging how the stood and sat around the outdoor furniture. A woman came out of house carrying a tray with drinks, and placed it on the table.

Again the scene changed, and the kid he saw held onto a different car door handle while talking to the driver. The driver wanted to go, the engine was at idol, then he moved the car ahead slowly at first, eventually speeding up. The boy held on, but finally couldn't keep up, he fell and was dragged until he let go.

He looked at his knees and how his pants were torn showing some road rash and blood. He rolled over and grabbed his leg, holding it, groaning, then saw the palms of his hands scabbed and bleeding as well. As he stood the car drove away, faded, and disappeared around the corner.

Now the images and scene changed again, and Michael found himself looking at an old three story brick house. The first floor had a three window design feature that extended outward, a porch on the right that led to the backyard with side entry door for the kitchen on the left. The driveway encircled the house leaving plentiful parking for family events.

Across the street was a stone church completely built of different colored stone from the ground to the top. To the left was an open field with a huge oak tree smack dab in the middle, and beyond was a school made of brick, across the street to the left of the school, another church.

The same man who had the camera was there taking pictures in front of the church of a boy dressed in a blue suit, a few alone, a couple with a priest, for the his first communion.

Now he was sitting on the window by the three window alcovecrying for some reason, then he left the house, crossed the street, and climbed one of three pine trees in the school playground. The boy sat on a branch watching his tears dropping down into the sand creating what looked like small explosions.

Why is the boy crying? Something bad must have happened, but what? Why can't I see what it is?

Again the scene changed and he was in the back of a truck with some furniture and other household items. *Someone is moving?* The truck stopped at a gas station to buy gas, but the driver had run out of money and traded his wrist watch for gas. I'll be back to get the watch later today, the man said.

Who is this guy, and where is he going with the furniture?

The truck pulled into the driveway of a ranch style brick house with a big yard and wooden fence on the right. Between the fence and house was a birch tree, and in front of the house there was an apple tree, and a maple tree with a big yard and wooden fence on the right. Between the fence and house was a birch tree, in front of the house there was an apple and a maple tree.

Now there was a swimming pool, a shallow end for small kids, and the deep end with two diving boards. Lifeguards posted around the perimeter were on duty the whole time. They blew the whistle for break time, that's when everyone had to get out of the pool, and sat on the edge kicking at the water.

Across the street there were two baseball fields, and a football field. A small food car with a long line of kids waited to buy hotdogs, candy, and pop. The kids parked their bikes in front of the pool in the space between the tennis court and pool. Baseball and softball tournaments were held in the summer, so the crack of a bat echoed during the day.

THOTH

In a dreamlike trance Michael stared straight ahead while his body was being forcefully projected forward like a missile confronting an endless vast space. The unknown cold cosmos surrounded him in glowing starlight, flashing and moving in all directions at incalculable speed. Without knowledge of the destination it led him on course, and flying with the precision of a bullet, to somewhere, someplace, somehow.

With no time, and not even the slightest chance to think or make any decisions, the bright beams of light surrounded him, bending and twisting as he got ever closer to a larger glowing revolving light changing in size and radiance. This pulsating hum echoed all around within a modulating wave of light that sent some sort of signal out to whomever could accept it.

Watching ahead, and while examining the knuckles on the back of his out stretched hands was a reflected mirror image of his face changing from a child to a teenager, an adult, and back to a kid. Then finally he stopped, and was left floating in the surrounding and endless time of space. Feeling alone and out of touch with life he tried to get his bearings, but all that seemed hopeless at this point. Then unexpectedly out of nowhere a synthesized voice radiated out from the air surrounding him like waves of water. It echoed similar to the sound of an old hand-held transistor radio speaker.

"Why are you here? Why are you here? Why are you here?"

"I knew that would be the question," he said, then thought, *I knew that's what would be asked.* Now why would I know that?" Michael whispered. "Have I been here before? *I think so.*"

"Yes, you have been here on many occasions to ask for my assistance and seek my counsel," the voice said. "I've always provided you with information that you could use to help find your direction, and for whatever reason, maybe it's just disbelief because you continue coming back to ask the same questions again and again."

"I always feel disbelief. Certainty brings the end, or start of something new."

"Perhaps the end you seek is never really clear, and why you always hesitate at key times. Why don't you accept what's being offered to you? I'm not sure why you can't take the last and final step. I'm not sure you can make the decision."

"Yes, bits and pieces are coming back to me, and I vaguely remember some of this now," Michael said with a relief that he understood, remembered a little, and had a grasp on what was happening. "I'm still not clear on what I've been offered though. Could you share that with me once more?"

Then a deep forceful voice spoke out from what seemed to come and be originating from not one but all directions. As he looked right the voice trailed from behind as well, the voice from all around flowed toward him no matter the direction he faced.

"Do you remember what you heard about the God of knowledge, and how through measurement, thought, logic, magic, this particular God, the scribe of the underworld, maintains all good and evil in the universe? Shrines and idols have been built for this God in many places; he's praised for being the author of all knowledge that ever existed from then, now, and forever. He is called Thoth or Moon God, or known as the producer of the light from darkness, inventor of the system to measure time and his focus is everywhere. Would like to meet Thoth?"

Then Michael said, making an attempt at humor, "Do I need an appointment?"

"The voice echoed back, "Scoff you do my friend

because this is who you are, and cannot fully grasp what's happening now. You still haven't been able to connect any of the dots as of yet, even though you've done this, and been here many times."

"I don't know about connecting dots because I can't see any dots. Do you mean stars are dots? If so, how do I, or how can I connect the dots? and see Thoth?"

"You can't see Thoth at this time because you are not ready."

"Not ready? Why not? When will I be ready? What do I need to do to prepare for this auspicious encounter? How do I get ready?"

"I can only say you will know when you are ready."

"Okay, can you tell me who you are? How do you know Thoth?"

"I'm your friend," the voice said. "Actually more than a friend and I know everything there to know about you. And I mean everything."

"How can you know everything about me?"

"Because we have talked to each other a lot, and we've had this same talk many times. I think after our conversations you only retain parts of what we've discussed, and nothing remains in your memory because you want to forget. That will change the longer you stay here. Soon you'll know all there is to know. Soon you will decide to take the next step, soon you will know what to do, and never turn back to your previous life."

"Where am I?" Michael asked. "What is this place?"

"It's amazing you don't know the answer; it's so simple. You are in your own mind, in your own soul, in your own your essence," the voice said.

"You're on a journey to places only heard by humans in rumors, legends, and myths. The mythological stories that are part of old history, and ancient tribes that have carved clues in stone, but even stone does not last forever, but some stone is special and has a memory, so the knowledge is passed on, and a few who possess this certain kind of particular information can do things that are theoretically unthought-of. Some think of it as just lost forgotten lore."

"Have you ever been human?" Michael asked.

"I'm the voice inside of you, so does that make me human? It may sound like an outside echo, but it emanates and comes from within you."

"What is this entity, not sure what you're trying to tell me?"

"Only you understand," the voice said. "No one else can hear it, only what the voice would say before it spoke. And some things he remembered how, what, and why they had happened. There was a time before time known by humans.

Then waves of images that looked like familiar structures of buildings flashed by like a slideshow. There was so much different architecture in each image, but only in view for the shortest time, and appearing only once. When Michael opened his eyes he was looking up to a blue sky, then he looked forward tracking with his eyes the twisting trail that had been made by a sled on previous trips sliding down the steep hill of snow. In front and behind were kids on sleds doing the same, sliding down the hill, excitement in their blaring voices.

How old am I? he thought.

On the side of the hill to the left was a brick building and a church.

That's the first school I went to.

The sled reached the bottom and stopped. Michael sat on the sled taking in the view, remembering the day, place, and things that had happened. A bell rang a few times as he watched the kids walk back to the brick building without hurry. He closed his eyes, and after opening them he was sitting at a wooden desk in a classroom, some papers with sketches of buildings and animals.

Now he was floating in space again, flying at high speed forward again into a vast unknown
place. As lights flashed glowed and reflected, he thought, *Where am I going? Can I choose the destination?*

The voice said, "Remember what I told you," the voice said. "You are the voice, and it comes from within you."

***

Now he was on a school playground heading toward a big oak tree going home after class. As he walked noticed that he began changing from a child into an adult, and when he saw the old three story house where he lived was all grown up. Michael stopped a moment before crossing the street and looked at the house and wondered what he would find inside.

After crossing the street he ventured into the house looking over everything. In the living room there were paintings hanging on the wall. All in all there were ten paintings of figures clad in robes. Michael stepped in front of each painting examining each one carefully, but the faces were obscured by shadows from hood that covered their heads.

"I've seen these figures before," he said, "but where? Why can't I remember?"

Then a woman's voice hummed a soft melody, and spoke in an unfamiliar language.

"I know that voice," Michael said. *It's Sue!* "Sue, where are you?"

"I'm standing right next to you."

"Why can't I see you?"

"We're in different worlds. You're on earth, and I'm on Rim Stone."

"Rim Stone? Where is Rim Stone?"

"It's in another dimension, a time that existed ages before there ever was a solar system as we know it, or planets that we all study and know."

"What is going to happen now?"

"You're finally going to Rim Stone like you have wanted many times before and this time succeed. Go to the house, find your way to the room at the top of the stairs, and meet with all of the figures that you see in the pictures. You will discover which one seeks control of Rim Stone. Stop them, find the book of knowledge. You have been chosen to ring the bell!"

BEDTIME STORIES & DREAMS . . . BOOK NOTES

When it came right down to it, and like everyone else Michael's age, he was just a regular kid just growing up living out his dreams at least so he thought. Hungry Point, where he lived near the Mississippi River, was always a permanent memory and image in his mind.

Throughout the time of his youth and what he remembered, or had been told from the onset, began to write down most things as a story in a journal. These stories varied from the perspective of a young kid to an old man.

In the beginning when he started writing, they, the stories, were variations on what was told to him by his grandfather at bedtime, hence the subtitile -Bedtime

Stories & Dreams. Again like any kid at first he believed the stories without question, but as he got older thought some were over the top, and made up by his grandfather. Soon the stories became meshed into his own dreams, connected with images, memories, characters he seemed to know, and actually recall.

Now as an adult he looked back to his youth, the memories, adventures, crisis, accomplishment, events, and things associated with this life. Why were his dreams so vivid? Why, why, why, why, why was always a question he had asked himself.

As he read over what he'd written; realized it came from a well of endless time. A collection of dreams and memories saved and banked, free for anyone with the wherewithall to access, employ or mold to one's deepest desire. A truely open source of knowledge for anyone to gain access, like the air we breathe. All around us, but taken for granted by most.

Over time the dreams became wild, an unreal reality in their own way that seemed out of control, but with its own unknown purpose. As far as Michael knew he was just living a ordinary life that included school, then hopefull going onto to study architecture at a college, or maybe joining the Army like his grandfather and father.

But that was only on the surface, what he really wanted was to direct or act in movies. He was interested in photography, which was a way to stop events and time with pictures and images. There were many paths to follow at this point in time, and these were all open to him. Deciding and making the effort to strive for accomplishment is what he understood, and everything was his to choose and decide. And when he realized he could do anything, the world of dreams took over and was unlimited.

His so called grandfather, and father both had been in the military as far as he knew, also from what Poppi and Moses had told him, it was an exciting, and possibly, dangerous life. Poppi started in the mason busineess after his service, he opened a shop and embarked on building with stone. But looking back when the chance to join the military came up, his dad and grandfather jumped at the opportunity, and seemed his destiny as well.

The job they had in the service involved building and repairing military structures, but also involved developing a network which Michael as a kid didn't fully understand. The job also involved traveling to Army bases, and occasionally Michael went along with Poppi, so watching him probably sparked and created the interest to become an engineer. It also planted the seed to enlist, infuencing him while growing up, and helping decide what he should to do in the future.

Not until he was older did he feel he'd come from somewhere far away, and as a baby, then young child, had no memory of the early events. But now he wanted to look for his birth parents, and this urge became an important goal in his life even though his grandfather had told him his parents had died in an accident.

He couldn't let go of the adopted parents idea, but had no documentation, and was never given any information. Michael was starting from scratch, didn't know their real name or if they were alive, just completely clueless, but wouldn't give up the idea.

The biggest surprise for him came when Sue's real parents, or actually her father, found her. This happened after recieving a letter from a detective, then meeting her father, and accepted a job at his company.

First there was an interview for a position at one of the largest IT companies in the world, and after meeting her dad who started and owned RIM, was told the company was interested in hiring her.

After applying for the job at RIM Inc., there was a call for her to go in for a second interview. Only the best candidates were chosen to work at RIM. If an applicant received a second call chances are they already had a job; the interview was a formality, and her father running the company didn't hurt her chances either.

After being hired at RIM, Sue began working on a project called, Mannequin. She couldn't talk about it, and in total only a few at the top had knowledge of all information connected to the project.

Sue usually worked late, was beginnning to act more distant, and not spending much time with Michael. She had tried to get him to work at RIM, telling him the job and company were fantastic, but he had no interest. He continued to work as a mason building with stone, and wrote more embellishing with bits about his dreams.

He would go to the apartment, sometimes just stay there on days to write. The room on the third floor seemed to play a part and influence his writing. There was something about that apartment on the third floor that left him confused and curious.

Michael sat at his desk in the apartment, and looked up at the ceiling after hearing the echoes of a bell.

I've heard that before, but where?

The bell sound continued and vibrated through Michael, and the room so intensely that he had to get up and move around. He could feel energy flowing through his body. Curiosity had him walk out of the apartment and follow the bell sound.

He made his way up the creaky narrow steps up to the door of the room at the top. Standing there with the sound attracting him closer like a magnet.

Then the door opened a crack, someone inviting him into the room, but didn't see who. Michael raised his hand, and pushed open the door. The bell sound stopped, and it was quiet, more than any kind of quiet he'd ever experienced.

"Hello," Michael said, and opened the door to an empty room.

"Anyone here?" he said in a low voice.

From a long hallway a small boy entered the room. Light shone on his face as he stood at the the other side of the room, then smiled.

"Hello," the boy said. "Thank you for coming today."

"Your welcome I guess. Who are you? Do you live here?"

"Please come closer," the boy said.

Michael stepped forward into the middle of the dark room, turned and said. "I've seen these people, characters, or beings in my dreams." He scanned the large canvas window like paintings that hung throughout space.

"How about me? Have you seen me before, or remember me?"

Michael stared at the boy. "You look a little like me when I was a kid."

"Funny you say I look like you because I am you."

"What?" Michael said. "You are me? What did you say? What?"

"Yes, and I've waiting here for you. I never grow old. Actually, I'm your transportation. I'm your vehicle."

"My transportation to where?"

"I'm here to take you to Rim Stone."

"Rim Stone? Where's that , and how does that work?"

"Using the formula to sound the bell. It's what that trinket you've been wearing around your neck this whole time is for."

Michael raised his hand and clutched the amulet. As he squeezed, it became warm, and a glow around his body vibrated with the echo of a bell as the room blurred.

***

Title for a third book could be Stone Men, Stone People, Stone Nation, Stone something. I've decided on the title, maybe, Rim Shadow or Stone Shadow . . .

I think I'll call it - RIM STONE —

Ideas for stories appeared in my mind, and I'm not sure where they come from, but feel like old memories. Then a thought came while writing down my ideas.

Sleep to dream, die so dead, wake to live a memory left in one's head.

***

Book III 'RIM STONE' Bedtime Stories - Dreams & Memories.

I first saw a dead human at seven years old during a funeral and thought - What happens to all of the knowledge that a person accumulates over a lifetime?

I fear no death because I've seen it many times. There are so many things that we learn over the years. If I were to write down everything, could I finish?

Are dreams & memories lost forever or floating in the air waiting for someone to carry on?

Reading books and learning more about dreams, what

is possible, and how your life could change. After fire purifies the ground, the sun rises from the horizon, and the dead return to life on a wind carrying the scent of life.

Generations living and growing from small clans populate the world as we know it, and is the world now, since time began to be recorded. The path leads to answers starting with the last war of death of destruction and conquest. The purpose forgotten, peace and harmony a distant memory, only a shadow of it remains.

One can't imagine the death and destruction from such war. Even the most powerful weapons we know of are nothing compared to what happened at this event.

***

Michael parked his car, and watched people walk through a door up narrow stairs to a pool hall. After years of playing pool at Kick's he had gotten fairly good, played in a few tournaments, but never for one that offered a fifty-thousand dollar prize. After seeing the ad for the tournament was compelled to enter, and now that he was there in the pool hall felt the electricity of the room.

The lights were low except for over the tables. Neon lights on the wall glowed blue, red and green. The pool hall was on the second floor of an old building with brick interior and exterior walls. There was a bar in the center of the space, and TV screens hung around the room. An old pay telephone sat in the back, all of the tables were being used, the sound of balls making contact snapped, and the tournament was slated to start in a few minutes.

"Hi, I'm Michael Colt, should be on the list to play."

The guy behind the bar looked down the list of names, running his finger as a guide. "Here you are," he said. "This is your schedule, and names of players in your group."

"Great, thanks." Michael said, then went to his table, and got his cue ready to play. He looked the table over, then breaking the balls, watching them rolling and spinning seemed similar to the solar system. The only thing different was planets didn't collide that much, at least he couldn't remember experiencing or seeing that.

Michael lined up to break the rack again when the table vibrated, the room spun, and he was in another dimension. Everything waas black, and quiet. He had know idea what was happening, but soon memories from the past returned. Ancestry, birth, and boyhood times, floated through his mind.

He was a human he thought, and had been for many generations, well travelled, and the word Nabataean came to mind, but where or what happened before was a distant thought. He remememberd traveling on foot, by horse, camel, ship, train, and plane. There were wars, business deals, meetings, subjects studied, and they all bubbled to the surface.

***

RIM STONE turns without hesitation powered by the SKRO, a magnificent engine with ten spokes from the center to the rim, each controlled by a WIX. The Rim is so vast that to imagine it would drive a mortal mind into scatter letting it drift into the welkin.

During this time the WIX, a creature with human form, stays in their domain. They gather at times to the SKRO to find the unknown and pass on power. The unknown is a human on earth with a connection to the WIX.

At the SKRO in the center, the WIX are locked in a trance, which is their way to see the unknown, who is the one that their power will be transferred to. If power is not transferred to the unknown it goes to the nearest WIX. As the layers of the RIM expand and contract during this time natural disasters occur on earth until all of he unknowns are chosen, and all of the WIX are replaced.

One of the WIX craves all and total power of RIM STONE, and takes steps to achieve this desire during the time of FRAHAZ. It's Ralk's turn to entertain the WIX during FRAHAZ, so all the WIX gather at his realm.

At this time all will change forever once all power is transferred to Ralk. If transferred to an unknown, Ralk will be stopped. Epag, Cadra, Abo, Gohl, Morana, Osrar, Tura, Uzura, Yapiz are aware and unaware of Ralk's plan even though they are of one conscience mind during the time of FRAHAZ.

Each WIX has a fortress to safeguard their power and transfer their power to an unknown.

Moss Moat that absorbs intruders.

Razor Ice shreds intruders.

Shadow Wall, invader becomes part of the wall.

Spinning Rings captures anyone leaving them in an endless cycle.

Trap Doors that lead to an endless maze.

Steam Fog that boils invaders.

Ripping Wind tears intruders to pieces.

Waterfall Needles turns anyone into a pin cushion.

Bottomless pits keep invaders falling forever into darkness.

Starlight that blinds intruders driving them mad

He stands behind, his hand reaching to grasp at the shoulder if the volunteer makes it through the trap. He looks at the moat covered in dry moss and a weak point and a way to get through. He takes a vine in his hands, and begins to climb slowly at first testing the strength.

The unknown looks above and sees . . . the goal in front.

Now, Michael looks out in front of himself, and sees space, just empty space. He doesn't know where he is, but does know where he wants to go.

TO

RIM STONE

BEDTIME STORIES AND DREAMS

Grandfather's bedtime stories aren't as innocent as they seem, but those dark tales could be a young man's only hope. Now to transform the onset of events he must alter the past.

DREAM KILLER Book I

THE TRIBE Book II

RIM STONE Book III

www.jsiwicki.blog

infojsiwicki@gmail.com